His hosts called for the couple to kiss—

A.J. looked stunned, and Shelby almost fainted. *Oh no!* her mind screamed. She didn't kiss men she didn't know, especially not ones like him. She should never have hurried over to confront him. Following her instincts was one thing, kissing a total stranger was another.

Her chattering, scrambling thoughts ran off in all directions when he drew her into his arms. Raising her onto her toes, he bent his head.

Make this look good, his eyes warned.

Don't make me do this, hers begged.

Then all thought ceased the instant their mouths touched and sensation took over....

Patricia Knoll, "when facing the imminent arrival of birthday number thirty and baby number four," decided there had to be more to life than changing diapers. She produced her first Harlequin Romance a few years later. Raised in a copper-mining town in the American West, she's always been fascinated by interesting characters and the stories they have to tell. And she's always loved books—the things with "new worlds to become lost in." Now she creates new worlds, too—ones with love and humor and happy endings.

Books by Patricia Knoll

HARLEQUIN ROMANCE
2902—GYPSY ENCHANTMENT

Don't miss any of our special offers. Write to us at the following address for information on our newest releases.

Harlequin Reader Service
901 Fuhrmann Blvd., P.O. Box 1397, Buffalo, NY 14240
Canadian address: P.O. Box 603,
Fort Erie, Ont. L2A 5X3

Always a Bridesmaid

Patricia Knoll

Harlequin Books

**TORONTO • NEW YORK • LONDON
AMSTERDAM • PARIS • SYDNEY • HAMBURG
STOCKHOLM • ATHENS • TOKYO • MILAN**

ISBN 0-373-02961-6

Harlequin Romance first edition February 1989

To my husband, Kyle,
who gives me ideas

CHAPTER ONE

REJECTED!

Shelby stared at the gold-embossed letterhead.

"Insufficient credit!" she sputtered. Her blue eyes skimmed down the page, disbelieving, then angry, then outraged. "Well, maybe I don't have credit, but I've got cash!"

Across the room Mary Featherstone looked up from her sewing machine. She appeared to be buried in yards and yards of the peach-colored chiffon she was using to create four bridesmaids' dresses for a neighbor's upcoming wedding. Seeing her daughter's incensed expression, she removed the dress pins from her mouth and stuck them back into a tomato-shaped pin cushion. "What did you say, dear? What's wrong?"

Shelby waved the offending letter at her mother. "I've been turned down for that empty shop in Spanish Court by Mr.—" she glanced down at the bold black signature scrawled across the bottom of the stationery. "At least I guess it's a mister—A. J. Court. How cute," she said, sarcasm edging her voice. "He named the mall after himself."

"Oh, Shelby," Mary gasped. "Turned down? And you were counting on it so."

Shelby slapped the envelope from Court Properties against her palm. "So were you and the rest of the family. It would have been perfect for our business, with the florist, caterer and baker all right there.''

"It was such a good idea, too." Mary's softly rounded face took on a dreamy look. "A business that arranges weddings, everything from the gowns to the reception."

Spurred by the disappointment in her mother's voice, Shelby shook her head. "We're not giving up! All our plans are made. With me arranging things and the whole family getting involved, I know we'll be a success. And Spanish Court is the perfect place."

The Moorish-style mall had just opened in an affluent section of Santa Barbara. Its clientele consisted of the up-and-coming young professionals who lived and worked in the area—exactly the type of customers she needed.

"Shelby, you know your father and I offered to co-sign for you on the lease and let you use our credit rating."

"No, Mom." Shelby roamed a few paces across the room. "I appreciate the offer but even though the family is going to be working with me on this, I want to get the lease on my own. I may not have credit, but I've got my savings and the money from Great Aunt Laura. Surely that's enough to make the needed alterations and pay the rent until I get the business going." Clutching the letter, Shelby stabbed the air with it. "I'm going to get this man to change his mind!"

"Shel—by." Mary drew her name out in a warning tone. "What are you going to do?"

"I'm going to call him." Shelby's bare feet slapped against the hardwood floor as she hurried to the kitchen.

"Don't do anything you'll regret," Mary called after her.

"Mom, you and Dad have always taught us to follow our feelings, to go with our first instinct. That's what I'm doing." Shelby snatched up the phone and punched out the number she had seen on the letterhead. "Don't worry, I'm just going to *talk* to him."

"And say what?"

"That we've got money to pay the rent; we'll be successful, he doesn't have to worry...."

Shelby's convincing arguments frothed like soap bubbles until the receptionist came on the line and reported that Mr. Court wasn't in.

Shelby slumped in disappointment. "Where can I reach him?"

"Miss, it *is* noon," the frosty voice intoned. "Mr. Court is at lunch."

"Where?"

"I'm sorry." The secretary's voice echoed, faded, then returned. "He's out of the building—glad—a message."

"What? Could you say that again?" Shelby frowned. What was wrong with the phone? She looked down at it in disgust, then hugged it closer to her ear. This was a terrible connection. Phantom voices seemed to be on the line. When the voices faded, then became louder, her eyes widened. Of course, she thought. The secretary probably had a hands-free phone. If she turned her face away from it, her voice faded and the speaker picked up all sounds in the office.

A male voice was saying, "...take you out to lunch. Erica's okay? The seafood is terrific and the boss likes us to patronize—"

"No," a woman answered quickly. "A.J. is there—something important brewing."

Shelby gasped with delight at her unexpected good luck. Erica's was a new restaurant in Goleta, just north of Santa Barbara.

"Miss, did you wish to leave a message for Mr. Court?" the receptionist asked.

"Never mind," Shelby answered quickly. "I'll call back later. Goodbye."

She rattled the receiver onto the hook and dashed through the house to her bedroom. "I'm going out for a while, Mom. I intend to talk to this Mr. Court face-to-face." She grabbed her purse off the bed and was headed down the hall when her mother called her back.

"Dressed in shorts and a tank top that don't match?" Mary asked, waving her scissors at Shelby's outfit.

"The stains match," Shelby pointed out with a cheeky grin as she ducked back into her bedroom. "They're from the wood refinisher I've been using on the desk for my new office. Besides, Mr. Court probably wouldn't notice unless my clothes had dollar signs printed on them. I'll bet A. J. Court is a hard-faced old curmudgeon," she fantasized aloud, snatching off her green-striped top and sending it flying across the room. It landed on the lamp shade, knocking it at a crazy angle. She slithered out of her red-flowered shorts and kicked them under the bed. "I'll bet he's about ninety-five years old, bald, with a big cigar stuck in his mouth."

"Just because he turned down your application doesn't put him in league with the devil," Mary reasoned. "He probably has many wonderful qualities. You should wear your blue dress."

Shelby rolled her eyes heavenward, smiling ruefully at her mother's way of jumping from the dreamy to the practical without even stopping for breath.

"Court could have at least considered my application a little longer." Shelby removed her new blue silk dress from its hanger and slipped it on. The color turned her eyes the hue of sapphires. The shirtwaist style fit beautifully, and the clever pleats Mary had designed disguised the hips Shelby was convinced were too full.

She slipped on high-heeled sandals, darkened her long lashes with mascara, ran a brush through her short brown curls, then glared at her reflection. Court might feel justified in turning down the application when approached by someone who looked like a pixie, she thought, brushing her curls back on each side. She knew she couldn't let her looks matter. She was out to do battle, not win a beauty contest. She rustled around in her drawer for matching tortoiseshell combs and slipped them into her hair.

Her crisp dress, neat hair and businesslike manner would help give her confidence. Unfortunately, nothing could be done about a mouth that was too wide, eyes that dominated her face, and a nose that was too small to balance her other features. By only a little had she escaped the usual Featherstone plumpness. Her oval face lent even more accent to her wide blue eyes.

"Goodbye, Mom," she called, snatching up her purse and dashing for the door.

"Be careful," Mary called out. Or was it "Be tactful"? Shelby wondered, as she closed the door and hurried to her Volkswagen Rabbit waiting at the curb.

She started the car, swung it onto the street and zipped down the hills to the freeway.

In less than twenty minutes she was at Erica's. Shelby pulled into the parking lot and sat staring at the restaurant. Built like a greenhouse, it had big windows and skylights that reflected the sun.

The righteous indignation she had felt was beginning to cool. What if Mr. Court was as bad as she imagined? She pulled a tissue from her bag, wiped her suddenly damp palms, stuffed it back into her purse, took a deep breath and squared her shoulders. "What's the worst he can do to me?" she asked herself as she slid out of the car and locked the door. "Blow cigar smoke in my face," she concluded, "and have me thrown out on my ear."

An elderly couple getting into the car next to hers gave her a startled look. Shelby answered with a wan smile, and headed for the entrance. She had come too far to let panic send her fleeing now. A. J. Court would *have* to listen to her.

Inside the restaurant's plant-filled foyer, she was met by a hostess dressed in a dark red suit of raw silk. The woman was stunning, with thick black hair that was pulled back in a braided chignon. The style emphasized her classic high cheekbones and deep-set eyes, while the warmth of her smile enhanced her elegant looks. Her age could have been anywhere between thirty and fifty.

The hostess's welcoming appearance drew Shelby up to her full five feet, two inches and inspired a brilliant smile. "Mr. A. J. Court, please."

The woman's expression warmed even more, transforming somehow from politely welcoming to delightfully conspiratorial. "Oh, of course. Please come right this way," she said, turning toward the dining room. "He was getting worried about you."

Stunned, Shelby blinked at the woman's retreating back, unable to believe her good luck. Court had a lunch appointment with a young woman! Never one to look a gift horse in the mouth, Shelby followed. "I got hung up in traffic," she fabricated.

"I told him that was probably what was wrong. He was ready to call the Highway Patrol to find you."

"Well, I'm here now," Shelby said heartily, her eyes darting around as she tried to decide which of the men in the room was A. J. Court.

"He'll be so relieved." The hostess wove her way past the other diners with Shelby trailing along behind her. "He's been here for a while...making preparations. He's so particular, wants everything exactly right." The woman looked back over her shoulder. "And he's so handsome."

Shelby had started to walk toward an elderly, cigar-smoking gentleman sitting near a cluster of leafy palms across the room.

"Handsome?" Her gaze swung ahead to where a dark-haired man sat alone at an alcove table shielded by plants. He was dressed in a tailored black suit, a white shirt and a black tie. He turned as they approached and Shelby looked into the coolest green eyes she had ever seen. The old saying about carrying a long spoon when supping with the devil popped into her mind.

From the hostess's manner, Shelby realized Court wasn't waiting for a business rendezvous, but a romantic one.

"Here she is." The hostess presented her young charge with a flourish. She stepped aside for Shelby to pass, favored them with a misty smile and glided away.

"Hey, wait a minute, Carmen," a deep voice protested. "This isn't—"

Knowing she had to do something quickly to avoid being thrown out, Shelby launched herself at the man who had half risen from his chair. "Darling! I'm so sorry I'm late." She wrapped her arms around his shoulders and gave the startled man a hug.

He reacted by sitting abruptly, jerking back and glaring up at her. "What the devil do you think you're doing? I've never seen you before."

Quickly, Shelby pulled out the chair opposite him and sat down. "I know I'm not the person you're expecting, Mr. Court. But if you'll just listen to me for a minute, I promise I'll leave before your date gets here."

As she talked, Shelby's misconceptions about A. J. Court were rapidly reforming themselves into reality. Ninety-five? This man wasn't over thirty-five despite the lines that rayed out from the corners of his eyes. He was lean and handsome in a harsh way, with angled cheekbones and straight dark brows that looked surprisingly delicate on his masculine face. She bet he never smoked cigars as she had imagined or did anything else harmful to his health.

But he seemed every bit as hard as she had expected.

Her impetuous courage almost failed when he stared at her for several seconds before answering.

"Miss, my date is already overdue." His voice was very low and precise. "She'll be arriving any minute, so you had better talk fast. I would have you thrown out of here, but I don't want to embarrass the owners. Who are you, anyway?"

"My name is Shelby Featherstone."

His gaze sharpened.

"I see you remember me."

"Yes. And the answer is still no. I won't reconsider."

"Why not? I've got money."

"You may have cash right now, but you have *no credit*," he said. "What happens if your business loses money and you can't pay your debts? I suppose I would be expected to allow you to stay in Spanish Court for free?"

She shook her head quickly, vehemently. "Of course not! I know I'll succeed. You would always be paid on time."

"What kind of business is it, anyway? La Grande Affaire... seems a bit theatrical, don't you think? So does your name, for that matter."

"It's my real name!"

He glanced at his watch, signaling his impatience. "And what is your *real* business? From the title, I'd guess it's something I don't want taking place in my mall."

Shelby gasped. Did he think she was going to sell pornography or run an escort service? "I'll be arranging *weddings*." Her voice trembled with outrage. "Just like it said on the application."

He shrugged. "Whatever you say. What are your qualifications for running such a business?"

"I've been a bridesmaid in five weddings," she answered with a firm nod. "My three older sisters and two friends."

He stared at her in astonishment before he threw his head back and hooted with laughter.

Shelby looked away, embarrassed. Her lips pursed as she waited for him to get over his outburst.

In spite of her wish to disappear inside the leafy fern beside her, Shelby couldn't help allowing her gaze to stray back to him. She was intrigued at the way laughter changed his face. The firm lines softened, his green eyes sparkled, a dimple indented the left corner of his mouth.

When his laughter finally wheezed into silence, he gasped, "Miss Featherstone, being a participant in a wedding is a great deal different from attempting to create a business of arranging them."

"I know that, but I *did* help arrange them," she answered tightly. "I've also worked in a florist's shop for five years, and I've taken several business classes at the university."

"You think that qualifies you to open your *own* business? How many clients do you have?"

She shifted, smoothing the skirt of her dress with restless fingers. Her thick lashes fluttered downward. Her lips pursed again. "One," she admitted. Her gaze shot up boldly, "But I'll have many more. This kind of business succeeds by word of mouth, you know. And I need to be in a good location and look success-ful before I can attract more clients."

"Perhaps so, but not in Spanish Court."

Of all the pigheaded, stubborn, impossible men! Shelby was forming a new set of arguments when the hostess appeared by the table with a telephone.

"I'm sorry to interrupt, Alex." She cast apologetic glances at both of them. "But this caller said it was urgent."

Court leaned back, allowing her to set the cordless phone down by his elbow. "Hello?" he barked into the receiver as the hostess moved away.

Shelby was amazed to see his face soften into a smile.

"What's the problem, *darling*?" His eyes lifted to Shelby, deliberately challenging her. "What's holding you up?"

Trying to appear as if she wasn't listening, Shelby glanced around the restaurant, admiring the plant-filled decor and rich, dark colors. Unconsciously, her fingers straightened the place setting before her, then wandered to the rim of the salad bowl. She plucked out a lettuce leaf and began nibbling it unconsciously, indulging her lifelong habit of eating when she was nervous.

"What do you mean you can't get away?" His face settled into a frown. Shelby felt sorry for whoever "darling" was. A. J. Court obviously was not pleased with the change in plans. She picked up a shred of carrot and popped it into her mouth as she studied him.

Now that she looked more closely, she could see that his crow-black hair had the faintest dusting of silver. In another ten years it would look very distinguished. She wondered if the graying was hereditary or caused by stress, like the deep lines that were now bracketing his mouth. Did he ever lighten up and see the joy in life? He had laughed, but it had been in derision, not pleasure.

"I expected you here. I had this thing timed down to the minute. You were going to— No, dinner tonight is out. I've got that meeting with Charleson. No, no, it's all right. I'll call you later.'' He hung up and speared Shelby with a look.

He put a time limit on lunch? she thought in amazement, picking up a tiny cherry tomato and popping it into her mouth. "Bad news?" she asked, then winced at herself for asking such a dumb question. The man looked as if he could spit nails.

"Nothing I can't handle," he answered with a flinty look. Under his breath, he muttered something unintelligible.

Shelby was glad she wasn't the date who had stood him up. She wasn't sure she would ever have the nerve to face him again. Her fingers returned to the bowl and a slice of cucumber followed the tomato to her mouth.

The hostess came to remove the telephone. As she turned away with it, she gave Shelby another warm smile. Shelby had the feeling that the hostess knew something about her—a secret the two of them shared. They had never met before, but Shelby was pleased that the woman seemed to approve of her. Enthralled, but mystified, she nibbled on another lettuce leaf.

"Now, where were we?" Court asked. He picked up the water glass at his elbow and took a sip.

His hurry-up tone snapped Shelby out of her daydream. "You were about to rent me the space in Spanish Court," she supplied cheekily.

"No, I wasn't."

"Mr. Court, I can make a success of La Grande Affaire."

"What assets do you have?"

"A strong back, a flair for organization, a supportive family and enough capital to start and keep me in business for several months."

An unwilling smile edged his mouth at her fervent tone. "And a lot of persistence. I mean, what kind of stock, supplies, et cetera do you have?"

Again Shelby's fingers sought the salad bowl before her. She toyed with a cherry tomato for an instant, then lifted it to her mouth. She chewed and swallowed before answering. "All I'll need are some comfortable chairs, low tables, some plants. I'm refinishing a desk...."

"Sounds like you'll need a decorator."

"My sister, Charmaine, is one," she said quickly, her spirits buoyed by his interest. "At least she works for one, and she can get the things I need wholesale."

"What else do you have?"

"My brother-in-law, Mark, will build the fitting rooms. Sample books of invitations and announcements will be provided by my sister, Sienna, who works for a print shop. My mother and my sister, Lindy, will make the gowns the clients request. I've located several unusual sites for outdoor weddings. My little brother, Creig, will photograph them as well as take pictures of chapels, reception halls, flower arrangements and bakery goods," she finished triumphantly. She picked up the water goblet before her and took a sip.

"It sounds like you and your family have everything planned."

Shelby knew she could hear a "but" coming. She leaned across the table and held out her hand, palm up, her eyes pleading with his. "Oh, don't turn me down, Mr. Court," she begged. "This business will be a success if given half a chance. You, better than any-one, know what kind of people patronize Spanish Court. Most of the clientele are wealthy professionals who would want a really stunning wedding, but don't have enough time to prepare it." She straightened her back and held her hands wide apart. "Why, the aver-age visitor to the mall spends over two hundred dol-lars a visit."

A. J. Court frowned as he picked up his water glass and took another sip. "How do you know so much about it?"

"Well, I did research, of course," she answered. "I spent days watching the clientele and talking to the store owners about their customers."

A strangled sound came from across the table. Court snatched up his napkin and coughed into it. "You're the one the security man stopped because he thought you were casing the mall for a robbery!"

"Oh," she said in a small voice, her gaze skittering away from him. "You heard about that, huh?" Her fingers strayed back to the salad bowl. Another cu-cumber slice found its way to her mouth.

"Yes, although he said he didn't get your name and that we didn't need to worry about you." Court looked as if he doubted that now.

Shelby didn't dare tell him she thought the security guard, Gary, had approached her to flirt and that they had dated a couple of times since then. In fact, Gary was the source of most of her information about Spanish Court.

"Uh, well." She paused, then she looked back at Court and plunged into her argument again. "I've done all the research and background and prepara-tions I can possibly do, *and* I've got the money to make the alterations and pay several months' rent, even if I don't have credit.''

Court sat and stared at her. His gaze was fixed on her but had an unfocused intensity that told her he was deep in thought.

Coming from such a big family, Shelby knew how to negotiate to get what she wanted. She also knew when to be silent and wait. Impetuous she was, without a doubt, but she wasn't stupid. She knew her chances of convincing him rested on the next few seconds. Nervousness fluttered in her stomach. Absentmindedly, she picked up the salad fork and began eating in earnest. The few bites she had eaten had whetted her appetite. The salad was crisp and delicious, with pine nuts scattered through it and a dressing flavored with ginger. Beside the plate was a napkin fluted into a bird of paradise shape. She reached for it to spread across her lap.

"What the hell are you doing?"

Startled, Shelby looked up from the bowl, her hand clutching the napkin. Court was scowling furiously now, not in thought, but in anger. "Why, I," she sputtered, choking down a cherry tomato. "The salad was just sitting here, and I, uh—no lunch and..." She frowned in confusion. He had already watched her take several bites. Why was he suddenly so upset?

Court reached across the table and snatched the napkin from her. With lightning motions of his fingers, he began unfolding it. "Where is it?" he muttered in disgust.

Shelby's hand flew to her throat as she watched him.

"Aha!" He lifted something from the folds and held it up.

It was a diamond ring!

Shelby's eyes grew enormous as she looked at the glittering stone, then at the hard-faced man holding it. She said the first thing that came to her mind. "Why, Mr. Court, isn't this a bit sudden? We just met!"

CHAPTER TWO

"MISS FEATHERSTONE, this obviously is *not* for you," A. J. Court said coldly, dropping the ring into his pocket.

Shelby's tongue clucked with sympathy. "You were going to propose to your date today, weren't you? And you put the ring in the napkin so she would find it, didn't you?"

A faint show of color started at the collar of his crisp white shirt and washed up his face like a tidal wave. "Well, not—"

"Oh, how romantic. Does she like surprises?" Shelby shrugged. "What woman wouldn't love a surprise like this?" she asked on a soft breathy laugh, a wistful smile lifting the corners of her full mouth.

Court's breath seemed to catch as he watched her rapt expression. For an instant an answering smile threatened to break the straight line of his mouth. He jerked upright, clearing his throat. "Well, now, where were we?" he asked, glancing around.

Something across the room caught his attention. "Oh, no," he muttered, turning back to her with an exasperated look. "I knew I should have gotten you out of here sooner." His hand shot into his jacket pocket. "Here," he demanded, pulling out the ring. "Put this on and pretend you're in love with me."

"What?" Shelby's shoulders recoiled against the back of her chair as if he had struck her.

"Just do it. You've forced yourself on me and made a wreck of my lunch."

"Me!" Shelby gasped. "It's not my fault your girlfriend couldn't make it."

He ignored her protest. "The least you can do is help me out." He grabbed her left hand and began jamming the ring onto her finger. It wouldn't slide easily, so he dabbed the corner of his napkin into his water goblet, wet her knuckle and began shoving the ring into place.

"Pretending to be in love with you would probably take more acting ability than I've got," she fumed. "Ow!" she yelped when he finally succeeded in forcing the ring over her knuckle.

"Hush," he commanded. "*Act* happy."

"With you scowling at me and my finger turning blue?"

"Something else will be blue—and black—if you don't help me out."

"All right, all right. Does this mean I get to rent the space in Spanish Court?"

"Hush," he hissed, rising to his feet, a dazzling smile lighting his features.

Shelby gaped at the change in his face. The irritated expression had been wiped away, leaving him looking happy and relaxed. The lines of his angular features smoothed almost into boyishness. She didn't know what to think. The impression she had gained of him so far had been that of a single-minded man with no warmth or sense of humor. But he had changed so suddenly, he couldn't have surprised her more if he had leaped up and started tap dancing on the table-top! He must have a good reason for what he was doing, she thought, but really, the man was wasted in real estate. He should have been an actor. She turned in the direction of his gaze.

The hostess, Carmen, was coming toward them, pushing a cart on which rested an ice bucket. It held a bottle of champagne. Behind her, supported by a cane, walked an elderly woman who was as classically beautiful as Carmen. Her thick, snow-white hair was pulled back in a chignon like Carmen's. As she passed through the dining room, she nodded to many around her. Shelby was reminded of a queen greeting her subjects.

Watching the two women approach, Shelby realized that the hostess had given her those conspiratorial looks because she had known exactly what was going on. Obviously it was very important to A. J. Court that these women think everything had gone well.

The two women, especially the older one, possessed a commanding presence that virtually drew Shelby from her chair as the small procession neared their table. The woman had deep-set dark eyes and skin that made Shelby think of fine rice paper. She held out slim, elegant hands to Court.

"Alexander, is everything well?" she asked in a breathily husky voice, her bright eyes darting from him to Shelby.

"Very well, Erica. She has agreed to become my wife." His deep voice rumbled with sincerity and satisfaction.

Knowing a signal when she heard one, Shelby lifted her hand and flashed the huge diamond. "Isn't it lovely?" she squeaked.

The woman clasped her hand and laid it along her own softly wrinkled cheek. "Oh, Alexander, this is wonderful." Tears filled her eyes. "Your mama would have been so proud. I'm sorry she didn't live to see this day."

"So am I," he answered, his mouth curving in a gentle smile that brought out the merest hint of his dimple.

Shelby was touched. The woman, apparently the restaurant's owner, must have ties to A. J. Court that went back many years. She saw him not as the powerhouse businessman he was but as a man she had known since his childhood. A.J. gazed fondly at the women.

"And what is your beloved's name?" Erica asked.

Shelby felt instant tension in the man beside her. A.J. went very still and he turned his head slowly so his intent stare was directed at Shelby. He had forgotten her name! Gulping furiously, she swallowed the urge to giggle.

"Shelly Featherstone," he said, looking triumphant that he had remembered. "This is Erica Martinez. You've met her daughter, Carmen."

"My name is Shelby." She stressed the *B*. Her voice came out an octave higher than usual. "He loves to tease."

"Yes, he does," Erica agreed, her eyes shimmering with pleasure. She looked back at A.J. "You've done so much for us, Alexander. We want to repay you with this," she gestured toward the champagne bottle. "And lunch is on the house. We're so honored that you brought your lovely young lady to our restaurant."

A.J. looked chagrined. "Erica, that isn't necessary...."

"Of course it's necessary," Erica scolded gently. She turned to Shelby. "He gave us everything, has done everything for us. This restaurant—a dream I've had all my life—wouldn't exist if not for him."

"Really?" Shelby asked, bemused. "He gave you— *everything*?"

"He's so modest that he probably didn't tell you," Carmen broke in. "We had little capital or credit, but he sold us this property and arranged a loan for the construction."

Court looked so uncomfortable at having her know of his philanthropy that Shelby couldn't resist favoring him with a sweet smile. "Is that right, darling?"

"That's right, honey," he answered through his teeth.

"You're a prince." She fluttered her eyelashes at him.

Court flashed her a look that said he would deal with her later.

The women smiled at their bantering. "You were right," Erica told her daughter. "Alexander has met his match."

Shelby felt ashamed of the way they were deceiving these two lovely women. A.J. shifted and cleared his throat, making her wonder if he didn't feel the same. She turned questioning eyes to him. Why was he doing this?

As if he sensed her confusion, A.J. looked at her and away, then smiled at Erica, his eyes suddenly alight with a calculating gleam. "And now it's time for you to repay me."

Erica blinked. "Why, Alexander, we've never been late with our payments."

"That's not what I mean. Do you remember the bargain we made a few months ago?"

Cheeks flaming red, Erica nodded. "I suppose you're going to collect now? I should have known when Carmen told me why you were here today."

"A promise is a promise."

Puzzled, Shelby looked from one to the other.

Carmen took pity on her. "You two are making Shelby feel left out. Really, Alex, you should have warned her. A few months ago Mother's doctor said she had to quit smoking and take things easier."

"I've worked all my life—" Erica broke in.

"And smoked since you were twenty," Carmen added dryly.

"Dr. Dodge expects me to quit working and smoking just like that." Erica snapped her fingers, a look of outrage in her dark eyes.

"Cold turkey," A.J. added.

"And you haven't done either one, Mother," Carmen scolded, then added to Shelby, "Alexander made her promise she would quit. She said she would when he got married."

"I thought I was safe. After all, Alexander is getting very close to middle age. I thought he was a confirmed bachelor." Erica sniffed.

A.J. smiled dangerously at her barb. "Oh?"

"So, I thought he would never marry. Obviously, I was wrong. He must have found the right woman in you, my dear." Erica treated Shelby to a smile that made her feel even worse. "And besides, you two aren't married yet," she finished triumphantly.

"As good as." A.J. drew Shelby close to his side. "Erica, you're leaving tonight for your vacation, and I want you to quit while you're gone. We don't plan to allow smoking at our reception, do we honey?"

His hand slid up her arm, and he clasped her shoulder, warming her through the blue silk sleeve. Shelby shivered involuntarily. "No," she said, her breath catching. She knew it was all an act, but his touch was deceptively loverlike. It took her a moment to gather her thoughts and recall what they were discussing. "It sounds like you're outnumbered, Mrs. Martinez."

Erica leaned on her cane and looked from her daughter's smile to A.J.'s triumphant grin. Her lips pursed. "I feel fine. Dr. Dodge worries too much. He's the most joyless man I've ever seen."

"You promised...." A.J. reminded her. His face held a stubbornly caring look as if he planned to go on arguing with Erica for the remainder of the afternoon.

Well, well, Shelby thought, A. J. Court did have a soft spot. And he had a good reason for deceiving these two sweet ladies, but she was very curious to know why he would go to such lengths for them. "It was a moment of weakness." Erica's breath caught suddenly, and she went into an alarming coughing spasm that caused Carmen, Shelby and A.J. to reach for her.

"*That* was a moment of weakness, Mother. You're weakening your lungs. You promised," Carmen echoed A.J., placing her arm around her mother's shoulders. "Alex proposed to Shelby at our restaurant to be sure you couldn't get out of your promise."

"Also, I've made an appointment for you at The Stop Smoking Clinic in Reno for tomorrow morning." A.J. drew a business card from his pocket with the information written on the back. "The program's all paid for."

"Don't disappoint them, Mrs. Martinez," Shelby added, reaching out to squeeze her arm. A.J. flashed her a startled look that she met with a serene smile. Mischievously, she added, "A.J. has gone to more trouble than you know."

"A.J.?" Erica asked. "Is this a new nickname, Alexander?"

Shelby blushed. To her, the initials fit him best.

A.J. looked amused. "It appears to be. Don't change the subject."

Erica looked at the three of them, then sighed. "All right. I did promise. But I think it's unfair of you to do this just as I'm leaving for my vacation."

"It will be easier," A.J. insisted. "A month at a lodge on Lake Tahoe, no cigarettes, good food. You'll be in perfect health when you get back."

"I'll be a crab," she said querulously, her silver brows drawn into a frown. "I wouldn't do this for anyone else."

"Neither would I," he answered, with a sidelong glance at Shelby who found herself gazing up at him and smiling at her partner in collusion.

The ladies exchanged delighted smiles of their own.

"Won't you join us for a glass of champagne?" Shelby asked. "To celebrate your decision—and our engagement."

"Coercion," Erica said firmly, shaking her head. "No, thank you. This moment is yours alone. We've intruded enough." Supporting herself on her cane, she stood on tiptoe to kiss A.J.'s cheek. "You must tell us when the wedding date is set."

A.J. looked nonplussed, as if in his careful planning he hadn't thought of that. "We haven't set a date yet."

Shelby came to his rescue. "Arrangements do take some time."

"Shelby just started her own business," A.J. said with a proud smile that only she and he knew was completely false. "She won't have a lot of time to think about wedding plans."

Oh, he thought he was being so clever, baiting her like that. It would serve him right if she set the date right then and there! Her full lips curved smugly.

A.J. caught her look and shifted warily. He slipped his arm around her and pulled her tightly to him. Shelby knew he wanted to forestall any mischief she might be planning.

"When the time comes you'll get an invitation," he promised, sending Shelby a meaningful glance before he turned away. "Carmen, I need to talk to you. I'll call tonight."

"Fine," Carmen said. "Now let us see you kiss your bride-to-be." Her face lit up with anticipation.

Erica beamed at the suggestion. A.J. looked stunned, and Shelby almost fainted.

"A kiss?" she croaked.

"Go on," Erica urged.

Oh no, Shelby's mind screamed. This man hated her. And she didn't kiss men she didn't know, especially not ones like him! She never should have hurried over here to confront him. Following her instincts was one thing, kissing a total stranger was another. Where should she put her hands? Not around his neck.

Her chattering, scrambling thoughts ran off in all directions when he drew her into his arms. Raising her onto her toes, he bent his head.

Make this look good, his eyes warned.

Don't make me do this, hers begged.

Then all thought ceased as sensation took over. The instant their mouths touched, her lips parted in surprise. The mouth she had thought harsh felt incredibly tender as it stroked over her own. The fleeting kiss finished almost before it began, but the sting of awareness shocked her, prickled its way down her body, melted her. She had to fight the need to slump against him.

When he lifted his head, Shelby thought she saw an instant of surprise quickly hidden behind his thick screen of black lashes. She blinked and looked around to see that Erica and Carmen were moving away, congratulating them and telling them to have a good meal.

A. J. Court's hands dropped away from her. "Sit down," he said grimly. "It looks like we're in for the duration."

He held her chair and she sank into it, still shaken. It took her several moments to put her feelings into perspective. It had been a kiss, that was all. Nothing to get excited about. She had been kissed before.

But not like that.

Shelby pushed the thought from her mind, knowing she couldn't be objective. Instead, she thought of the two women who were walking away. She wondered when A.J. would tell them the truth.

The thought of food cheered her. Fake engagement or no, she could always eat, and she knew the food at Erica's would be superb.

Across the small table, Court looked like a thundercloud.

"Does this mean the engagement is off after lunch?" she sighed, spreading her napkin across her lap. "And after all we've meant to each other, Mr. Court."

"Don't be coy," he growled. "I guess you might as well call me A.J. while we're here. After lunch, I want you to give the ring back and disappear from my life."

"I think you're being completely unreasonable. It's not my fault you were stood up."

He winced. "You've really got a way with words, don't you... Shelby?"

She didn't intend to apologize. "You didn't have to tell them I was your fiancée. You could have told them the truth."

He looked down, concentrating on smoothing his own napkin. "That I'd never seen you before and you forced yourself on me? Yes, I could have, but Erica and Carmen went to so much trouble, I couldn't spoil it for them—"

"And besides," she finished for him. "You knew it would be a way to get Erica to do something for her own good. I never would have suspected you of having an impulsive side."

His brows flattened in a scowl. "It wasn't impulse. I had planned it for some time. Unfortunately, my date couldn't make it."

"And I was a good stand-in. Now, aren't you glad I came?"

He still scowled.

"My father says it's good for people to follow their impulses. He says your first reaction is usually your best one." Her blithe smile faded as she recalled her impulsive dash to Erica's and what had happened since.

He tilted his head, nodding solemnly. "The idea of carpe diem—seize the moment. Funny you should say that. Turning down your rental application was my first reaction, and I was right."

It was Shelby's turn to scowl. She had neatly painted herself into a verbal corner. Unwilling to give up the advantage for long, she folded her hands in her lap and lifted her chin. "Erica is a lovely woman and so is her daughter. They must mean a lot to you."

A.J. shifted in his chair and leaned back as the waiter came to remove their salads. He opened the champagne and poured some into two tulip-shaped glasses.

"Our families were neighbors. Erica and Carmen were my mother's best—only—friends. They visited and cared for her every day before she died. I'll never be able to repay them for that."

"Where were you?" she asked, attuned to the emotion she heard behind his words.

"Slogging through the jungles of Vietnam." He picked up his fork and began eating, effectively closing that topic.

Shelby decided to let the subject drop, although she was intensely curious about him. She looked up as the waiter approached with a mouth watering assortment of seafood, and her eyes widened at the sight. This might be the shortest engagement on record, but she was going to enjoy the fringe benefits while she could. Her family was going to love this story. Shelby lustily worked her way through the lunch, trying the different sauces that were supplied with the meal. She closed her eyes in ecstasy over one particularly succulent bite of shrimp and opened them to see A.J. staring at her. He seemed to be fighting a smile.

"It's not very often I'm out with a woman who actually likes to eat," he observed.

"Including your fiancée? Is that why you ordered the salad, because that's all she was likely to eat?"

The left corner of his mouth edged down, emphasizing his dimple. "You know, you ask a lot of questions and make a lot of observations that are none of your business."

"Then why did you bring the subject up?" she asked reasonably. "My dad says you have a right to discuss anything freely if it's not likely to hurt someone's feelings."

"How very philosophical."

She shrugged. "Joe Featherstone may be a mechanic by trade, but he's a philosopher at heart." She looked around. "Is there dessert?"

Casting her a slightly incredulous look, he signaled a waiter for her.

She enjoyed the strawberry shortcake tremendously, but allowed herself only a few tiny sips of champagne. She still intended to talk business and needed a clear head.

Replete, she sat back. "I didn't want to spoil lunch by discussing business, but I want to know if you plan to rent me that space in Spanish Court?"

His face hardened. "I already said no."

Shelby straightened, prepared to begin her arguments all over again. "Listen, Mr. Court, you have no reason to..."

He looked pained as he rose to his feet. "Can we please talk about it outside? After you've given me the ring back."

"Afraid I'll throw it down and stomp on it?"

"How did you guess?"

"Just remember, wearing this wasn't my idea!"

"I'm beginning to think it wasn't one of *my* better ones," he grumbled as he pulled her chair out, took her arm and led her outside. In the parking lot he turned and held out his hand.

Shelby gazed down at the diamond for a moment. It was bigger than anything she would have chosen, but it caught the light beautifully, sparking with inner fire as she turned her hand in the sunshine. With a sigh, she moved to slide it off. "Oh, no," she breathed. "It's stuck!"

"What do you mean, 'it's stuck'?"

"I mean, stuck-stuck. It won't come off. My knuckle is probably swollen from the way you shoved it on."

"That's right, blame me," he growled, grabbing her hand. He tugged at the small circlet.

"Ow, you're hurting me!"

"I'd like to. Now what?" He looked back at the restaurant. "I can't ask them for help."

"Gee, thanks."

"We can't go back to my office. I don't want the gossip."

"We wouldn't want to shock the hired help," Shelby observed with asperity.

"Well, do *you* have any suggestions?" he snapped. Turning, he swept the sides of his suit jacket open and planted his hands on his lean hips.

"We'll have to go to my house," Shelby answered, nursing her sore finger. "My mom will know what to do." Her eyes brightened. "Maybe my dad has some axle grease we can smear on it to make it slide off easier."

He paled at that suggestion. "Hey wait a minute. That ring is a valuable investment."

Shelby started at his choice of words. His poor fiancée. Court would probably want to have the poor woman's left hand insured by Lloyd's of London!

"Come on," she said impatiently. "You can follow me. The sooner we get this over, the better I'll like it. After you rent me that shop, I don't want to see you again."

"What makes you think I'm going to rent you space?"

"My sore finger!"

His hand chopped through the air. "I'm not going to your house. This has been enough of a fiasco without involving your family, who are no doubt as flaky as you."

Shelby left him talking to thin air as she whirled and stomped to her car, dug out her keys and opened the door with a jerk.

"Be careful with that ring," he shouted after her, leaping into a dark green Jaguar.

"You're the one who stuck it on my finger," she shot back. She started her Rabbit and swung out of the parking lot. He cranked the engine of his fancy car and sped after her.

Within a few minutes they were pulling up in front of her family's modest home. Her father's truck was in the driveway, as well as Creig's souped up Camaro. Oh, great, now they would have an even bigger audience, Shelby thought.

Her parents and brother met them at the front door.

"Hey, Shel, what's happening?" Creig asked as he leaned against the doorjamb. His eyes, as blue as her own, took in the Jaguar parked at the curb and the grim-faced man towering over his sister.

"Well, I was out minding my own business, and look what followed me home."

"Shelby!"

"Sorry, Dad," she sighed. She waved one hand between her parents and the visitor. "Joe and Mary Featherstone, this is A. J. Court. A.J., these are my parents, and this is my brother Creighton. Creig to the family."

"Darling, isn't this the man you were going to see about the shop?" Mary asked, her fingers fluttering to her throat and her round face pinkening with concern.

"Yes, Mom, and it's a long story. I'll explain later, if you'll just help me get this ring off." She held up the huge sparkler.

Her dad's bushy salt-and-pepper brows shot up. "I can't wait to hear this one." He cast a wary glance at the man beside his daughter.

Mary looked at her youngest daughter in confused wonder. Although her parents had experienced many shocks while raising five children, Shelby knew this one had them reeling. She managed an apologetic smile.

Shaking her head, Mary took charge, hustling Shelby to the kitchen. She filled a bowl with ice and water to soak her daughter's hand. "This will take the swelling down a little, then we should be able to get it off with soap. Won't you sit down, Mr. Court? Would you like something to drink? A soda perhaps? Some iced tea?"

Shelby marveled at the graciousness her mother showed even when she was eaten up with curiosity.

"No, thank you," he said curtly. "As soon as I have the ring back, I'll be going."

Shelby could tell that her parents, usually the most amiable and garrulous of people, didn't know what to think of this reticent stranger in their home. An uncomfortable silence settled over them and Creig. She didn't try to break it. With her hand in freezing water, she really didn't feel like being sociable.

Their visitor didn't seem to be bothered by the silence. His eyes roamed the snug, homey kitchen and looked out into the dining room. One wall was papered in soft pastel stripes, but in the center of the wall was a gaping hole. Her father's current spare time project was tearing out the wall that separated the dining and living areas. She could just imagine Court's expression if she told him that Joe looked on this project as a way of tearing down "barriers of misunderstanding," an example he thought the world should follow to solve its problems.

Shelby's hand was growing numb in the ice water, so she pulled it out. Her mother led her to the sink, squirted dishwashing liquid on her hand and slid the ring off easily. Shelby slumped in relief, flexing her reddened finger as her mother hastily rinsed and dried the ring and handed it back to A.J.

"There, safe and sound." Mary smiled, her eyes bright with curiosity. A.J. thanked her, slid the ring into a small velvet bag he had taken from his pocket and pulled the drawstring tight. He slipped it back into his pocket and patted the flap down.

Shelby stared at her bare finger, her full lips curved into a gentle smile. She had never cared much for jewelry, but she loved the romantic idea of owning a symbol stating that somewhere in the world there was a man who loved her. She gave a thought to the woman who would receive A.J.'s ring. What was she like? Beautiful and sophisticated, no doubt. She wondered if Erica and Carmen would think the other woman was as perfect a match for A.J. as they had thought Shelby was.

A.J.'s face was serious as he turned to Joe. "I suppose you would like an explanation, sir."

Shelby started, realizing that her parents were viewing her dreamy-eyed look with a mixture of curiosity and alarm. She jerked upright and smoothed her expression into one of innocence. Taking a bottle of lotion from the windowsill over the sink, she poured some into her hand and massaged her sore flesh. Whoever his fiancée was, she must have small hands, she thought idly. That ring was tiny.

Joe tilted his head and regarded A.J. shrewdly. "Don't you think we deserve one? My daughter leaves with murder in her eyes, and comes back with the intended victim—and an engagement ring."

Shelby hurried forward. "I'll tell you all about it, Dad. I think Mr. Court would like to get back to his office." She took A.J.'s arm and began propelling him toward the door.

He went willingly, nodding goodbye to her parents.

At the front door she stopped and put her hands on her hips. "I'm going to send my application in again for you to reconsider."

"You can send it, but that doesn't mean I'll look at it," Court answered. "You're very determined to have your business in Spanish Court. The saints preserve me from stubborn women," he mumbled.

The scowl Shelby gave him hid the hurt she felt at his words. She was persevering, not stubborn.

"Wait just a darned minute." She poked a finger at the center of his perfectly knotted tie. "I went along with that trick you played on those two sweet ladies. I guess it was for Erica's good and you'll tell her the truth when she gets back from Tahoe. But you took a chance that they wouldn't find out the truth and you took a chance when you helped them build their restaurant. I realize it's different," she added quickly, "because you've known them for a long time. But you took a chance on me today in that restaurant. I could have told them everything and walked out since you'd already turned me down. Instead, I went along with your scheme because I thought it would help."

Despite her irritation with him, she remembered how important Erica's health had been to him. Shelby admitted to herself that she had *wanted* to help him.

A.J. stared at her for a minute longer, then his face softened. The corner of his mouth twitched, then spread into the first genuine smile she had received from him. He shook his head slowly. "All right, Shelby. I'll reconsider your application. Send another one to my office."

Shelby's stomach fluttered with excitement. She didn't know if it was from happiness or from seeing a glimpse of A. J. Court's better nature. "Thank you," she said softly.

He was staring down at her, the harshly handsome planes and angles of his face gentling. He didn't answer right away, but allowed his gaze to linger on each of her features—her eyes, which grew wider the longer he gazed into them . . . her short nose and finally her mouth, which began to quiver.

Shelby could hardly breathe. She felt as though the last breath she had taken was trapped in her chest. Her gaze dropped to his mouth, and she was lost in remembering the kiss at Erica's. She shivered.

Her slight movement drew A.J. up abruptly. His momentary look of tenderness disappeared as if blown before a blast of air.

"You're welcome—I think," he said coolly. "Goodbye, Miss Featherstone. It's been—interesting."

Shakily, she gathered her composure. "Goodbye, Mr. Court. I trust I'll be hearing from you soon."

He shook his head in reluctant admiration of her determination. "Don't worry, you will." He stepped onto the porch and hurried down the steps.

"Oh, Mr. Court," Shelby called after him.

He turned back, his tufted black brows raised in question.

"I hope she says yes." As soon as she said the words, she wondered if she spoke the truth. For all his stubbornness, it was somehow pleasant to think of Alexander J. Court out there—available.

He looked puzzled for an instant, then lifted his chin in a quick upthrust. The gesture evinced his masculinity and self-assurance. "She already did." With an easy, gliding motion, he slid into the Jaguar and drove off.

Shelby felt a little sorry for the girl, whoever she was. Standing up to A. J. Court and gaining equality in their marriage wouldn't be easy.

She shut the door and turned around to see her family standing in the hall.

"All right, young lady," Mary said, her usual whimsical look replaced with one of worry. "Tell us everything that happened from the minute you ran out of this house.''

To allay her mother's fears, Shelby gave a humorous account of the events that led up to her bringing A. J. Court home with her, leaving out the kiss to avoid Creig's teasing. The memory of it, though, and the look A.J. had just given her out on the porch made her dizzy. She had never before met a man who affected her so strongly. She didn't know what to think of it.

"You made an impression, there's no doubt about that," Joe said, scratching his head. "Do you think he'll rent you the shop?"

"He'd better!" The more she thought about Spanish Court Mall, the more perfect the location seemed. "He doesn't think I can make a go of it."

"Maybe he found out you've had four different jobs in the past six years, Shel," Creig observed, as he slid into a living room chair and draped his legs over the arm.

"No, he didn't find that out. And besides, I held two of those jobs at the same time, and they all had to do with preparing for this one."

"Now, now, you two don't get started arguing," Mary insisted. "Shelby, Lynn Altman called."

Delighted, Shelby spun around. "She's home?"

"Has been for a week, but says she's been too busy to call."

"Yeah," Creig said. "Being the city socialite can really cut into the time you spend with your friends."

"Mind your own business, little brother," Shelby retorted good-naturedly as she headed down the hall. In her room she made herself comfortable on her bed and picked up the phone.

Lynn had been gone most of the spring and summer, so Shelby had seen little of her. The two girls had been good friends since grade school, despite the difference in their social position.

When the Altmans' housekeeper, Mrs. Moran, answered and said Lynn had just left, Shelby's smile of anticipation collapsed into disappointment.

"She asked me to invite you over Saturday night," Mrs. Moran told her. "She's having a party to welcome herself home and she was especially anxious for you to come."

Pleased, Shelby agreed and hung up.

"ISN'T THIS THE GUY you were engaged to for a couple of hours the other day?" Creig held up the newspaper he was reading and waved it in front of his sister.

Shelby was sitting at the living room desk, papers spread around her as she attempted to draft an operating budget for her first few months in business. Her two accounting classes hadn't fully prepared her for the realities of running La Grande Affaire. The tax laws alone were daunting. When it came to debits and credits, her mind spun.

The figures were all beginning to run together, anyway, so she pushed the papers away and faced her brother. He was draped in his usual sprawl across an easy chair.

"You mean A. J. Court? Why? Has he taken up sports?"

Creig would have looked insulted if he hadn't been too lazy to bother. "I do read other things in the paper besides the sports page."

"Yeah, the funnies and that sex therapist's column."

"Well, maybe I saw the guy in the funnies. That's the only kind who would marry you. Mom and Dad were thrilled for about ten seconds the other day because they thought they were finally going to get you off their hands."

"Ha, ha," Shelby mocked. "You were thrilled because you thought you might be getting my room. Now the picture please?"

Creig held the paper aloft and she got up to take it from him.

It had been three days since she had seen A. J. Court, and the memory of their crazy encounter hadn't dimmed.

His photograph was on the society page, included in a column about a benefit dance at the Museum of Modern Art.

Shelby studied him. He looked darkly handsome in evening clothes, and the woman beside him was exactly what Shelby would have expected. She, too, had dark hair, a dress cut almost to her navel, and what Shelby judged to be a pouty mouth.

The caption identified A.J.'s companion as Marla Gaines, a docent at the museum. Shelby was sure the woman must be his fiancée, but the picture's grainy texture made it impossible to tell if the hand wrapped around a wineglass wore the ring or not.

Lynn Altman occasionally volunteered her time at the museum. Shelby wondered if she knew Marla Gaines.

"That him?" Creig broke into her thoughts.

"Hmm? Oh, yes. It is. This must be his real fiancée."

No wonder he had been so sure she would say yes, Shelby thought. Marla Gaines looked ready for anything.

Appalled at her own cattiness, she dropped the paper back onto Creig.

"Are you jealous?" he taunted.

"Don't be ridiculous," she said, cursing the way her face gave away her emotions to her teasing younger brother. "I barely know the man. I'm curious, that's all."

"Uh-huh."

"Mind your own business."

"I am. La Grande Affaire—gosh what a sappy name—is going to involve the whole family." He stood and wrapped an arm around her neck, leaning on her.

Shelby tried to elbow him aside, but he captured her and held her as his prisoner—and crutch. Creig never stood without leaning against something, preferably something soft. He never stood if he could sit, and he never sat if he could lie down. He was undoubtedly the laziest person she knew.

"Family business? You're planning on working?" she asked skeptically.

"Sure. I'm going to volunteer to chauffeur the pretty bridesmaids to the church, or anywhere else they want to go."

"In your Camaro?"

He looked shocked. "Heck, no. You're going to have to rent or buy a limousine."

She jerked her arm out of his grasp and gave him the full benefit of her elbow in his ribs. "Not a chance."

"Oomph!" he grunted, massaging his side. "Hey, it's just a suggestion. You've asked everyone else in the family for suggestions."

"I'll consider your suggestions when they're worth listening to," she said, then turned at a familiar sound. "There's the mail! Maybe the rental agreement has come."

On the porch, she all but snatched the mail from the carrier as he was about to put it into the box.

There *was* a letter from Court Properties. She ripped it open and scanned the enclosed letter.

Her application had been denied. Again!

CHAPTER THREE

"I WOULD LIKE to see Mr. Court, please."

Shelby hadn't even taken time to change clothes but had hurried out wearing a hot-pink T-shirt tied up at the side of her waist and a pair of loose, white drawstring pants.

"Do you have an appointment, miss?" The receptionist at Court Properties looked at Shelby over the top of silver-rimmed half glasses.

Shelby smoothed her hands over the knot of fabric at her waist and wished that she had taken a minute to put on the pearl-gray suit her mother had made. She would have looked more businesslike and mature. Instead, her usual headlong manner had brought her to meet A. J. Court in clothes she would have worn to the beach. She noted the woman's name on a small wooden plaque at the front of her desk. "No, Miss Simmons, I don't but..." She smiled warmly. "Tell him his fiancée is here. I'm sure he'll see me."

The lady's eyes widened.

"I know I look different," Shelby chirped. "Newspaper pictures are so unflattering." She knew that even poor photography couldn't account for the fact that she was a great deal shorter and more rounded than the lady in the newspaper, and she had a head full of short, brown curls rather than a sleek black pageboy. She could only hope Miss Simmons hadn't been wearing her glasses if she had seen or met A.J.'s real fiancée.

Miss Simmons glanced down the hallway to her left. "He was out and I was away from my desk. He may have come in." She reached for the phone. "I'll buzz him."

"Don't," Shelby said hastily. "I'll just go right in. Don't bother to get up," she chirped when the receptionist started to rise to her feet. "I'll surprise him." Turning, she bolted down the hall to the door marked Alexander J. Court. To her relief no one came out of any of the offices lining the hall, and she was able to make it to A.J.'s door without being stopped. She glanced back over her shoulder at Miss Simmons and smiled. Miss Simmons frowned back and started after Shelby, but the ringing phone stopped her.

Well, she hadn't won any popularity contest there, Shelby thought. She hoped her impetuous entrance didn't create problems for the receptionist. It was too late to turn back now, she thought.

Before she lost her nerve, Shelby mentally assembled the persuasive arguments she had formed during the drive over. She opened A.J.'s office door, whirled inside, and shut it behind her.

It was empty.

Shelby slumped against the door, her hand still on the knob, and surveyed A.J.'s office. Miss Simmons had been right. A.J. *wasn't* in.

She heard a faint roaring sound and glanced vaguely toward the window to see if there was a fountain in the courtyard. She saw only plants. Shrugging, she turned back to survey the office. It was as beautiful and tasteful as she would have imagined.

The floor was carpeted in a dark red plush that blended beautifully with the subtly striped wallpaper and the conversation area couches upholstered in dark gold. A closed door to her right probably led into a conference room. Along the walls were cases filled with crystal.

Intrigued, she moved toward the first case. It seemed to hold a veritable zoo of miniature animals. The enchanting display included two bear cubs tumbling over each other, their expressions frozen in playful perfection. A lion appeared to be opening his mouth in a half yawn, half roar, as if life was too pleasant to bother complaining about. A tiger lay on his back, one paw raised to bat at a tiny butterfly suspended over his head. Elephants munched at slivers of crystal straw or had their heads thrown back as if to trumpet into the air. A chimpanzee hung gleefully from one arm, his saucy tail curled into a question mark.

Shelby moved to the next case. This one had abandoned the zoo theme for one just as fanciful. Circus performers from clowns to bareback riders ranged across the shelves, and Shelby became so enthralled in this new world she barely noticed when the roaring sound stopped.

Her eyes darting everywhere at once, Shelby studied the delightful array, wondering what kind of man A. J. Court was. He seemed like a hardheaded businessman upon first meeting, and yet he had been willing to do a lot to make Erica Martinez take better care of herself. His office, the ultimate in high-powered corporate perfection, had a winsome collection displayed along the walls.

It didn't surprise her that A. J. Court would have such an expensive and tasteful display in his office, but she was amazed that he apparently wasn't the least bit embarrassed to have his little boy fantasies out for all the world to see. The man was turning out to be more of an enigma than she had imagined.

She whirled around at the sound of a door being opened. Her eyes widened in horror when she realized the room she had thought was an empty conference room was a bathroom occupied by A. J. Court—who had been in the shower! A pair of running shoes and a jogging suit had been dropped on the floor, testimony to why he was showering in the middle of the afternoon.

Her frantic mind screamed for her to run, but her feet refused to move. Shelby's face grew pale, then red, and her eyes were huge as she gazed at him.

Clad only in a towel that reached from his taut waist to the middle of his hair-dusted thighs, A.J. stepped before the mirror. Shelby was mesmerized by the sight of his broad, bronzed back and the muscles that moved beneath his skin when he lifted a hand towel to wipe the glass. The thirsty terry cloth made a clear swath across the steamy glass, and Shelby could see herself—her shocked intense gaze and red face—in the moments before A.J.'s eyes locked with hers and he whipped around.

"What the— How did you get in here?"

With his black hair standing in spikes around his head and his green eyes furious, A. J. Court looked more devilish than ever.

"Miss Featherstone, what are you doing here?" he demanded, stalking across the office. Glaring, he stopped in front of her and planted his feet slightly apart. He put one hand on his hip and wrapped the other one around her upper arm.

Shelby fervently wished he wouldn't stand like that. He looked like some kind of primitive warrior—about to lose his loin cloth. And she *really* wished the feel of his warm, damp hand wasn't affecting her like a dose of raw whiskey.

Her tongue seemed to be too thick for her mouth. She couldn't force words past it. If she had been shocked before, it was nothing compared to what she felt having A.J.'s furred chest only inches from her nose. Her eyes enormous, she tilted her head back to look at his face.

"I was admiring your crystal," she blurted.

"What!"

"I—I mean I want to talk to you."

"You're developing a habit of showing up in the wrong place at the wrong time. Have you ever considered just using the telephone?" His fierce scowl brought his brows together in a straight line.

"Would you have talked to me?"

"Probably not."

"Well, then, it's a good thing I came in person."

A.J. sucked in his breath, an action that Shelby feared would send his towel plummeting to the floor. She kept her eyes firmly fixed on his face until his breath expelled in a long, patient sigh. Hers expelled in a long, relieved one.

"What do you want?"

Utterly embarrassed, she pleaded with him with her eyes. "Uh, do you think you could put on some clothes?"

One brow climbed toward his mussed hair. To her immeasurable relief, he let go of her arm. "No. You're the one who barged in here. You'll have to take me as you find me."

Her befuddled mind put the worst possible connotation on his words and she reddened even more.

He ignored her deepening shock. "I've got a meeting in twenty minutes and I have no intention of talking to my lawyer and my accountant wearing this towel. That means I'm going to take it off in a couple of minutes and get dressed. Now tell me what you want and then leave."

It wasn't an idle threat, Shelby knew. He looked determined. When, oh when, was she going to learn to think before approaching this man? "My application was turned down. How am I going to get the credit you insist I need if you don't give me a chance? Did you get started in business with a string of banks or other companies ready and willing to give you loans?"

His forehead creased in puzzlement as he looked at her. "No, I'll get to your—"

"Then why do you expect that of me?"

"More small businesses are started and fail now than ever before," he pointed out.

"Because there are more *people* than ever before. Mine won't fail. And besides, you owe me something for having gone along with that charade the other day."

A.J. gave a quick shake of his head. "This discussion is pointless. We've gone over the same thing before. Now you'd better go, unless you want to see more of me than you intended."

Shelby thrust out her chin. "If I go now, I'll just be back again. Look, does your company have a board of trustees I can talk to?" she asked, blustering.

He gave her a patient look, then his sharply handsome features took on a look of wicked amusement. "I'm the owner, Miss Featherstone."

"You're unreasonable, Mr. Court."

"You'd better go," he said, hands on his hips.

"This isn't settled."

His hand went to the top of the towel. "Yes, it is. I told you, I'll get to your application as soon as I can."

Now it was Shelby's turn to stare in puzzlement. "Get to my application? You must think I'm pretty naive."

He shook his head, settling a few of the spiky tendrils closer to his scalp. "Listen, I have people coming. I'll give you to the count of three to get out of here. One."

Shelby's chin lifted. "I'll be back."

"It won't do you any good. Two." His fingers sought the tucked-in corner of the towel.

"What would your fiancée think if she knew you had treated me this way?"

"My fiancée? *She's* not involved in my business. Three." He plucked out the corner of the towel.

Shelby fled with his laughter following her.

Outside the office she jerked the heavy door shut behind her and rushed down the hall. A few people looked up from their desks to see her streak by. She spied a drinking fountain in an alcove. Flushed and distraught, she ducked into the recessed area, took a big drink and splashed a little water on her flaming face. Gasping for breath, she straightened.

Never had she humiliated herself in this way, she thought morosely, blotting her face on her T-shirt sleeve. She had always leaped before she looked, but never had the results been so disastrous. The shop would never be hers now. A. J. Court would see to that. She might as well start looking at less desirable properties.

She took a moment to compose herself, pushed away from the drinking fountain and headed down the hall, head erect. Thank goodness Miss Simmons was away from her desk. Shelby didn't feel like answering questions. There would be plenty to answer when she got home.

She decided to delay that as long as possible. A hot-fudge sundae would help—maybe make it possible for her to go home and face Creig.

"YOU MEAN LUSCIOUS LYNN didn't invite the whole family to the party?"

"Creig, I didn't actually talk to Lynn, just to Mrs. Moran," Shelby explained none too patiently. "You're not really interested in Lynn's party. You just want to sample whatever the caterers have brought."

Creig leaned against the doorjamb of her bedroom and watched her put on her makeup. "What's wrong with that? The Altmans always have great food, and they wouldn't invite all those people if they didn't expect them to eat."

Shelby turned from her makeup mirror and gave her brother an amused look. "None of their guests eat like you do."

"Except you," he quipped, ducking out of sight when a mascara tube came flying at his head.

It was true, Shelby thought, retrieving her mascara from the hallway and shutting the door. Her depression over the way she had blown it with A. J. Court had sent her on a two-day eating binge.

Worried, she pinched her side. The small amount of flesh she could gather between thumb and forefinger didn't *seem* any bigger than it had a week ago, but she didn't dare get on the scales. She promised herself that she would go over to the pool at her sister Sienna's apartment building and swim every day. But right now her weight was the least of her worries.

She had looked at other available shops and offices, but none of them were as good as Spanish Court. It was probably her own stubbornness rather than a lack of suitable properties that was making it so hard, but it was impossible for her to give up her dream.

She had to hurry and find something, though. Her neighbor, Karla Barnes, was La Grande Affaire's first customer. She had taken a chance when she agreed to have Shelby and Mary make her wedding arrangements. Karla was frequently out of town on business and her fiancé was in the Navy, so Shelby had virtually been given free rein to make preparations. Because she had put so much trust in the Featherstones, Karla deserved the best; certainly a great deal more than having her wedding dress and her bridesmaids' gowns crammed into the den closet along with Creig's old baseball equipment.

Shelby slid her bathrobe off her shoulders and took her dress from the closet. Another of her mother's creations, the party dress was of dark red silk. The style was modest, sleeveless and high-necked. A row of perky ruffles started at her left shoulder, ran across her breasts, circled her waist and traveled down the skirt in a fanciful corkscrew that finally ended at the hem.

She brushed her hair back on one side and secured it with a rhinestone clip, allowing the nut-brown curls on the other side to frame her face softly. She slipped on gold high-heeled sandals and surveyed her reflection in the mirror.

Not bad, she decided. She wouldn't exactly set the world on fire, especially if she compared herself to Lynn, but she would do.

Shelby had given up comparing herself to Lynn by the time they had reached junior high school. While Shelby and their other friends had been battling acne and baby fat, Lynn Altman had sailed along with a milky complexion and a figure that seemed to flower in perfect proportion almost overnight.

For a while Shelby had been in awe of Lynn. Besides all that money, she had gone from beautiful little girl to stunning young woman with none of the usual adolescent awkwardness. Shelby quickly discovered that Lynn hadn't changed. Her basically sweet and accommodating nature was just the same.

The rapidity and smoothness of Lynn's maturing hadn't been the blessing Shelby had assumed it to be. Somewhat to her surprise Shelby discovered that the insecurities of adolescence served a purpose in preparation for adulthood. Without that preparation Lynn had spent her high school years wondering if people, especially boys, liked her for herself, her looks or her father's money. On the other hand Shelby knew by age fifteen that she would never get any taller, her freckles would never merge into a nice allover suntan, and her eyes would always be too large for her face. If people liked her, it was for herself.

After graduating from high school Shelby and Lynn had gone their separate ways, Lynn to a private college and Shelby to a series of jobs to prepare her for going into business for herself. They had talked on the phone or met for lunch a couple of times a month until a year ago when Lynn's father had died of a heart attack.

Mrs. Altman couldn't bear to stay in her home after the funeral, so Lynn had gone with her on a lengthy trip, then helped her buy a new home near her sister in San Diego. Lynn had probably returned to Santa Barbara to take a breather from her mother. She was an only child, and her parents' dependence on her had always been overwhelming. Shelby thought things were probably worse now that Mrs. Altman was alone.

Thinking of Lynn, Shelby's eyes narrowed. There might be another reason for Lynn's return. For more than a year Lynn had been involved in an on-again, off-again relationship with an Italian race car driver named Carlo Rosetti. The Altmans had heartily disapproved of him. The last time she and Lynn had talked on the phone, several weeks ago, the affair had been off. Carlo, it seemed, couldn't make a commitment. Lynn wanted a home and family.

Her thoughts were interrupted when Mary walked into the room and plopped an armload of laundry down on Shelby's bed. "Will you be late tonight?"

"No, not too late."

"You look lovely, honey." Mary reached out to fluff the ruffles on her daughter's shoulder as she frowned critically at her creation. "Is the fit all right? Not too snug in the bust?"

"I certainly have enough bust for it to be snug on," Shelby sighed. "The dress is wonderful, Mom, and you know it. You're just never satisfied with your own work, like any true artist."

Mary's fretful expression melted into a smile. "Thanks, honey." She fidgeted with Shelby's dress a moment more. "I never expected you to grow up to be so beautiful."

"I'm not beautiful," Shelby answered firmly, then held her hands up. "I know, I know—I am to you."

"Your father and I are glad to see you going out tonight. We've been worried about you. You've taken this business with Mr. Court too much to heart."

"He's unreasonable."

"Perhaps so, but you'll simply have to live with his decision and find another place for your shop. Or use our credit rating."

"I guess so," Shelby answered, her blue eyes troubled. "But I wanted to do this on my own."

"You have to have help standing on your own before you can learn to run."

Shelby giggled and gave her mother a hug. "Oh, Mom, I love it when you get philosophical. You sound just like Dad. Is that what thirty-five years of marriage does for you?" She swept her small evening bag up from the bed and gave herself one last critical look in the mirror. Laughter had brought a sparkle to her eyes and she felt more cheerful. She turned and gave her mother a kiss on the cheek. "You're right. It's time for me to quit moping."

Late-summer chill crisped the air so she grabbed her full-length all-weather coat and pulled it on as she hurried out.

Waving goodbye to her dad, who was working in the garage, Shelby slid into her Rabbit and started for the Altmans' home. It took her fifteen minutes to reach the section of Santa Barbara where exclusive homes, estates really, nestled among the hills.

Shelby couldn't honestly say she would have preferred growing up in one of the mansions set back behind security fences, but she felt a definite twinge of envy as she passed.

Her wealthiest relative had been Great Aunt Laura, who had lived very modestly. No one had expected her to leave such a sizable inheritance. Even split five ways, it gave each of the Featherstone children a nice nest egg.

The Rabbit hit a bump, rudely bringing Shelby back to reality. She might be envious of the homes but not of the road leading to them, she thought, wincing as she swerved around a pothole. Even the nicest streets weren't immune to last winter's heavy rains, not to mention a few small earthquakes that had rearranged the street's surface.

Shelby eased up on the gas pedal, but it was too late. As she rounded a corner, her tire hit a pothole and she heard the unmistakable clang of a rear hubcap falling off. She glanced in her rearview mirror just in time to see the shiny silver disk roll away behind her car and disappear into a clump of mustard weed.

Disgusted, she pulled over and stopped. Stepping from the car she hurried back about twenty yards and peered into the weeds that lined the road, fuming silently. The people who spent thousands of dollars on gardeners for their homes couldn't be bothered to cut the weeds along the road. In a more rational moment she would have admitted that it was really the city's responsibility to do so.

With a fat stick in hand, Shelby leaned over as far as she could and poked among the weeds, trying to estimate the path of the hubcap as it had spun away. The weeds were knee-high, dense, and all looked alike.

Leaning on her stick, she glanced back over her shoulder.

A convertible with several young boys in it whipped around the corner. Wolf whistles split the air as they sped past.

"They could have offered to help," she muttered, jerking upright in reaction to their whistles.

When she heard the sound of another car approaching, she didn't turn around but kept moving down the street, trying to keep her shoes clean while poking among the weeds with her stick.

As the car slowed then crunched to a halt on the graveled surface, Shelby stiffened. She wasn't sure she wanted help, after all. No telling what kind of pervert might decide she was easy prey.

She grasped her stick in a threatening manner. Cautiously she looked around then groaned in dismay when she saw it was the last person in the world she wanted to see.

"Going fishing?" A. J. Court asked as he stepped from his dark green Jaguar.

Shelby's heart gave a stupid little kick. He was dressed in brown slacks, cream-colored jacket of raw silk and a yellow open-necked shirt that enhanced his dark looks. He was darned attractive, but she already knew that. Insufferable, but attractive.

She fought down memories of their last disastrous encounter. Chin up, she turned back to find him standing directly behind her. "Good evening, Mr. Court."

"Oh, we're back on a formal basis, hmm?" he asked, his green eyes glittering with amusement. "I thought we'd gone past that stage since you've seen so, uh, *much* of me. What are you doing?"

Shelby refused to answer his barb but couldn't help the redness of her cheeks.

"I lost a hubcap," she said, dropping the stick and pushing her hands into her coat pockets. Being buttoned up to the neck in her practical beige coat made her feel self-contained and in control.

"I see." He looked back at her Rabbit. "Did you just come around that corner?"

"Yes."

"And hit that pothole?"

"That's right." She started to move away, head down, her eyes searching the weeds. He paced beside her.

"You're looking too far back."

"What?"

"You should be searching up there." He nodded toward the car.

Shelby saw the full-blown humor in his eyes. Oh, he was enjoying this.

"Don't be ridiculous. I looked in my rearview mirror and I saw it rolling away."

"Did you read the sign?"

She glanced around. "What sign?"

A.J. took her arm and led her back up to the Rabbit and pointed to the printed message on the side mirror. "Objects are closer than they appear," he read aloud. "You're looking too far back."

Oh, of course. How stupid of her. She ground her teeth in frustration and stomped down the asphalt. Her hubcap lay in plain sight in a patch of weeds only ten feet behind her car.

A.J. glanced down at her high heels and hurried ahead of her to pick up the hubcap. He held it up with a flourish. "I'll put it back on for you."

"Thank you so very much," she said, giving him a royally freezing look.

He led the way to her car, put the hubcap in place and pounded it with the heel of his hand. When he straightened, he dusted off his hands and regarded her with an inquiring gaze. "Don't you want to thank me?"

"I already did."

"But you didn't mean it." He swept the sides of his jacket back, placed his hands in the pockets of his pants and rocked back on his heels. His dark head tilted to one side and his darkly handsome face was arranged in a smirk.

What was the matter with him? He seemed elated to have caught her in a couple of uncomfortable predicaments. He was remembering her embarrassment in his office. She could see it in his eyes. She just wished she wasn't remembering it, too.

"Was there anything you wanted to ask me?" he went on. "Did you want to nag me about your application or admire my...crystal?"

"No," she answered, her shapely lips pulled into an unyielding line. "You've done enough for me for one day. Did you want anything more? To become engaged to me perhaps or jam a ring onto my finger?"

His superior look collapsed into a frown. "No."

"Then why don't we go our separate ways, hmm?" She wrenched the car door open and slid inside. Motor roaring, she sped up the street, leaving him standing, looking after her.

She should have taken the opportunity to ask him why her application had been denied again, but his know-it-all look had been too much. He probably owns one of these fabulous houses, she thought, glancing from side to side. Poor Lynn! He might even be one of her neighbors. Seeing him had almost ruined her anticipation for the party, but she was determined to enjoy herself.

But, darn it, why did she have to notice how good he looked.

Shelby's car swept through the Spanish-style wrought iron gates and pulled to a stop behind several others lining the circular driveway. Her little economy car looked out of place beside all the Cadillacs, BMWs and Mercedeses that glittered in the lit drive, but she stepped from it and strode grandly up to the front door.

She paused for a moment to admire the house she hadn't visited in over a year. Like many homes in Santa Barbara it was built in the Spanish style of architecture. Of white painted adobe, it resembled a hacienda ranch house of the past century, built as it was around a central courtyard and pool area that was as lush as any tropical jungle. Shelby knew that was where the party would be held.

At the door she was greeted by a smiling Mrs. Moran, who cried, "Hello, Shelby."

The housekeeper had been with the Altmans since Lynn was in junior high. Shelby studied the woman's trim figure and short stylish haircut. As far as she could tell, Mrs. Moran hadn't aged a day in the thirteen years she'd known her. With an envious sigh she stepped in and gave the housekeeper a hug.

"Hi, Mrs. M. You look wonderful, as always."

"Don't try to con me. The food is already out on the patio. You won't need to raid the refrigerator before the party."

Shelby laughed. "Ah, my reputation haunts me." She looked around at the people milling at the entryway and in the living room. "Where's Lynn?"

"Out on the patio surrounded by a crowd," Mrs. Moran said happily.

"That's nothing new."

Mrs. Moran laughed, moving Shelby aside gently to open the door for the next guests.

Inside, Shelby greeted several people she hadn't seen in a long time and moved toward her hostess.

As usual Lynn looked stunning in a sleek, figure-hugging white dress of silk knit and was the center of a large crowd of people. Once Shelby got close enough to greet Lynn with a hug, but they were immediately separated by a new batch of guests.

Shelby shrugged. Oh, well, maybe they would be able to talk later.

"Hey, lady, is this dance taken?" a voice growled in her ear.

Shelby sidestepped a couple who were making a beeline for the bar and turned to see Jeff Chambers, a friend from her high school days, towering over her. He was as tall, blond and handsome as ever and probably still didn't have one serious bone in his body.

"It's not taken if we can fight our way through the crowd to where the dancing is," she answered, nodding toward the end of the patio where a small combo was playing.

"Hey, I didn't play football for four years for nothing." Jeff extended one elbow for her to hold and the other to clear a path. In moments they were through the crowd and on the dance floor.

Shelby laughed up at him. "Why, Jeff, you have such a breathtaking technique!"

"Only one of many," he said, waggling his eyebrows at her and taking her into his arms. He looked around. "You know, Lynn may have more money than she needs, but she sure can throw a party."

"You sound like my little brother."

"Heaven forbid," Jeff said, shuddering. "I hope I'm past that age."

Shelby laughed as he twirled her around. She was glad to be with an old friend having a good time, and she lost herself in the fun until he took her through a particularly perilous series of steps. Gasping, she pulled away to tease him about his prowess as a dancer, but he was frowning into the crowd behind her.

"Hey, Shelby, do you know that guy coming toward us? He doesn't look too happy."

Shelby looked around, but since she didn't have Jeff's height advantage, she couldn't see over the crowd. "Maybe someone spilled a drink on him."

"From the way he looks, someone must have spilled a whole tray of them on him."

Shelby didn't have time to glance around again before she found herself being gripped from behind. A strong hand wrapped itself around her upper arm and a familiar baritone voice said, "Excuse me, I believe this is my dance."

Jeff seemed to pale at the dark-haired man with the grim face. "Uh, sure." He stepped back hastily, his pale blue eyes shooting questions at Shelby.

So much for the brave football hero, Shelby thought as Court swung her about. The dark red silk spun in a wide circle as Court pulled her to him.

She resisted, arching her body away from him, her eyes mutinous. "Court, I don't want to dance with you. What are you doing here?"

"Well, *I* want to dance with you," he said, his voice low and scathing. "I want to talk to you because I want to know what *you're* doing here!"

Shelby found herself being clasped tighter in his arms. His legs nudged hers, his body began to sway, and before she could pull away or protest they were dancing.

She threw her head back and glared up at him. "I don't want to dance with you."

"You're repeating yourself. Besides, it's too late. You're already doing it."

It was true. Against her will her feet were moving in perfect counterpoint to his. Her arm was curved around his sinewy shoulder, her body pressed against his muscled length.

"You've got more nerve than any woman I've ever met," A.J. muttered furiously in her ear. He forced a smile and nodded to a couple dancing near them. "Hello, Gary, Susan, how are you?"

Shelby was stunned, unable to form a coherent reply to anything he was saying. Her feet moved automatically with his.

He placed his jaw near her ear. "Don't say anything until we get away from this crowd. I don't want an embarrassing scene."

"I don't, either," she said quickly, wishing she had thought to say it first. She followed A.J.'s lead as he danced her toward a less crowded corner of the patio. Too slowly, as far as Shelby was concerned.

She looked up at his face, but it was turned away. He was concentrating on maneuvering them through the crowd. His jaw was set, giving more emphasis to his strong angular features. He was freshly shaven and the faint spicy scent of his aftershave teased her. The overhead lights caused blue highlights to glint in his black hair.

Vaguely Shelby noticed the other women looking at him. He was exceptionally strong and powerful look-ing. She was becoming uncomfortably aware of how much taller he was than she, how broad his shoulders were. It occurred to her that she could probably hide behind him completely. He would make a good shield.

Experimentally, she flexed her fingers against his jacket. They met the resistance of his hard muscles. Awareness sent a shaft of lightning skidding up her spine. Surely he felt it, too.

At the movement of her fingers he glanced down sharply, a question or comment ready on his lips. Whatever it was, he never said it. He stared into Shel-by's surprised face with a faintly puzzled intensity, as if taken up short by what he saw.

Her lips parted, Shelby waited for him to speak, but words never came. He only gazed at her, his glance lingering on each point of her face.

The muscles tightened at the back of Shelby's neck. Heat washed through her, flushing her cheeks. Her eyes grew slumberous.

A.J.'s arm drew her closer. Her knees bumped his. His feet stopped moving, as did hers. He took her hand from his shoulder and cupped it against his chest. She looked at her own hand, felt the raw silk against her fingers and his warm, faintly callused palm against her knuckles. Mystified, she looked into his face. He made her furious. He had denied the dream she had worked toward for so long. He made accusations and laughed at her. But when he touched her—kissed her—she trembled.

Shelby closed her eyes to break, at least, that contact with him and to deny what was happening to her.

When she opened her eyes again, A.J. was blinking as if someone had shone a blinding light into his eyes. His half-wondering expression chilled.

Shelby expelled a shaky breath. She had never been more aware of a man—or more frightened of that awareness.

She tried to remember what they had been arguing about. "What are you doing here?" She repeated the question she had already asked him twice.

He seemed just as anxious to hurry past the moment. He resumed dancing, but drew away so that they barely touched. "I'm the one asking the questions here, Shelby. First you show up at lunch, then in my office, then so conveniently on the road, now here. How did you know I was on my way here?"

She started to open her mouth, but he held up his hand. His voice ripe with exasperation, he said, "Never mind. Don't answer that. I don't think I want to know. You probably weaseled information out of my receptionist somehow. I swear I'm going to fire that woman."

"Don't you dare! She's never told me anything intentionally, and I'm not here because you are." Lifting her chin she sent him a haughty look. "I'm an invited guest."

"Sure, you are," A.J. snorted. "And I'm the hired soprano."

"I didn't know you sang," Shelby said sweetly.

His gaze darkened and his mouth pursed thoughtfully. "You know, gate crashing isn't going to make me look any more favorably on your application."

Shelby's eyes widened. "Favorably! You've already turned me down."

"And I'm beginning to realize more and more that I was right. Why didn't you start nagging me about the shop when we met out on the road? I could have turned you down again and you could have gone right back home. You wouldn't have had to stage that little 'lost hubcap' scene. I've seen more originality in old movies!"

"Staged it," Shelby squeaked, finally pulling away. She opened and closed her mouth a couple of times, unable to think of anything nasty enough to say to him. If they had been standing out on the terrace she might have pushed him into the pool.

"Well," he demanded. "What have you got to say for yourself?"

Before she could answer, A.J.'s attention was caught by someone across the room. His green eyes narrowed. Between one instant and the next he seemed to have forgotten her and their argument. "Damn," he muttered. "That's Randy Anderson."

Caught up in their argument, it took Shelby a moment to understand what he was saying. "Who? Oh, you mean the society columnist?" She looked around in confusion, catching sight of a tall, handsome young man with warm brown eyes and broad shoulders. He looked more like a sportswriter than a gossip columnist.

A.J.'s face had the same calculating look it had held when he was trying to convince Erica to follow the doctor's orders. Shelby stepped back, eyeing him warily, utterly confused by his sudden shift of interest. "What are you thinking?" she asked.

His gaze turned to her. "I didn't know Lynn had invited him," he said slowly, obviously turning some plan over in his mind, considering it from all angles and finding it pleasing.

"He attends a lot of parties. He may have come with someone else."

"Yeah, maybe." A.J. pulled his full attention back to her. He studied her puzzled expression. To Shelby's amazement he lifted his hand and ran a finger down her soft cheek. He watched her stunned reaction, his expression calculating. "I'm about to take a leaf out of your book, Shelby."

"What—what are you talking about?"

"Carpe diem. Seize the moment," he said watching her face. He let out a long sigh like a man who has seen something he wants and can't have it. "You know, Miss Featherstone, you've got the world's lousiest timing."

With that he turned and strode away just as the dance was ending.

More confused than ever and overcome with curiosity, Shelby followed and watched as he separated Lynn from a horde of guests. He drew her to one side where they talked in low, hurried tones. Shelby thought it looked as if A.J. was trying to convince Lynn of something. Lynn looked thoughtful as he spoke, then she gave him a radiant smile and threw her arms around him in a hug.

A hundred thoughts chased each other through Shelby's mind. A.J. and Lynn had to be friends, or he wouldn't be at the party. But they seemed to be more than that, and whatever he had said had made Lynn very happy. For the first time since seeing A.J., it struck Shelby as odd that his fiancée didn't seem to be around. With a twinge of conscience she realized she should have thought of that sooner. If only she could keep her wits around him!

She didn't have much time to dwell on that, though. A.J. was holding up his hand, calling for attention. The crowd quieted. Everyone turned to face him.

A.J. put his arm around Lynn's shoulders and drew her close to his side.

Out of the corner of her eye, Shelby saw Randy Anderson moving forward, his reporter's interest obviously piqued.

"When Lynn decided to throw herself a welcome home party, she didn't know it would have another purpose," A.J. said, looking down at Lynn and smiling. He took her hand and drew a deep breath into his lungs. Shelby felt as if all the air had been drawn from hers. She didn't know what was going on, but a feeling of dread grew in her. Her heart felt as if it was bouncing between her throat and her stomach. She was lightheaded with a feeling of inevitability when A.J. continued. "I . . . we decided to take this opportunity to announce our engagement."

As he spoke, A.J. looked directly at Shelby with an odd expression that seemed to be a mixture of defiance and regret.

Gasps and cries of delight rippled around the room. Guests applauded as A.J. leaned down and kissed Lynn lightly on the lips.

CHAPTER FOUR

"HAVE ALL OF YOU met my fiancé?"

The guests at the buffet table turned to Lynn to offer their congratulations.

Very carefully, Shelby set her overflowing plate down on a nearby table and took a minute to compose her features.

In the aftermath of A.J.'s announcement she had scurried to the buffet table. The other guests' raids on the food might have been prompted by hunger, but hers was due to the storm of conflicting emotions she was feeling. When had this come about? How long had Lynn and A.J. known each other? she wondered. Her curiosity and confusion were tangled with a touch of anger at both of them.

Lynn was supposed to be her friend, but she hadn't said a word about being engaged. Shelby's anger at A.J. was far less justified. He didn't owe her any explanation and it certainly wasn't his fault that she was attracted to him. But, darn it, who was Marla Gaines? And where was that ring?

Forcing what she hoped was a pleasant expression onto her face, she turned around. Lynn was smiling radiantly up at the tall dark man beside her. They were a striking couple, Shelby thought. The difference in their coloring was as impressive as their looks. Their height was above average, drawing even more attention and comment. They would have beautiful, tall children, Shelby thought with a pang. Unconsciously, she straightened her spine. "Hello, again, Mr. Court."

Lynn's soft brown eyes looked puzzled. Her gentle fall of blond curls shimmered as she turned her head. "You two know each other?"

"We've met," A.J. answered as he drew Lynn to his side and placed his arm around her waist. His eyes were on Shelby. Did they hold a warning? she wondered. He didn't honestly think she would hurt her friend by mentioning that scene in the restaurant, did he? Or her disastrous visit to his office? Or her lost hubcap? He might, she concluded. He obviously didn't know that she and Lynn were old friends.

Just as she hadn't known that he and Lynn were in love. Life could get very complicated, she thought with an inward sigh.

"We just met recently," Shelby said.

"Oh, good, then Alex knows about your new business."

More than he wants to, Shelby thought cynically, her eyes going to his watchful face. "We've discussed it."

"Wonderful, because I want you to make all the arrangements for my wedding." Shelby gasped and A.J. started. He jerked his arm from Lynn's waist and stared at her in surprise, but she rushed on. "It's going to be quite a large wedding. I'll have six bridesmaids. And I want you to be one of them."

"Wait a minute, Lynn...."

"I don't think that's a good idea," Shelby chimed in.

Lynn stopped speaking, the radiance beginning to fade from her smile. "What's wrong?"

"I think you'd better slow down on these arrangements," A.J. said. "You don't want to rush things." There seemed to be hidden meaning behind his words, but Shelby was too involved in her own objections to decipher his tone.

The shock of the announcement, followed by Lynn's request, was too much for Shelby. Nervously, she reached out and plucked a canapé from the plate she had set down. She didn't even taste it as she popped it into her mouth and swallowed it almost whole.

"I don't know, Lynn," Shelby put in. "I don't have things quite organized. You might want someone else." Involuntarily, her eyes met A.J.'s. A scowl marked his forehead with triple indentations.

"But I thought things were coming together so well. When I called the other day, your mom said you had found a shop and everything." Lynn's beautiful mouth turned down in an engaging pout.

"Well, things didn't work out quite like I'd planned."

A.J.'s face was grim as death as he looked at her. For an instant Shelby wanted to defend herself. She hadn't done anything wrong. She wouldn't apologize. She certainly did not want to arrange their wedding, even though it would be one of the social events of the year and generate wonderful publicity for La Grande Affaire. "I haven't exactly found the right place yet," she amended, grasping at straws. "I've been looking at properties."

Lynn turned a pleading face to A.J. "Can't you do something for her? Don't you know of anything available?"

"Well..." He hesitated and Shelby could see him struggling between indulging Lynn and giving in to Shelby's demands. Whether she had a shop or not, he wouldn't want her making his wedding plans any more than Shelby wanted to do so!

"I know." Lynn laid her hand on A.J.'s arm. "There's an empty shop in Spanish Court. You see, Shelby, he owns the mall. Anyway, I saw a vacant shop. Wouldn't it be perfect, Alex?"

Feeling as if someone had given her a heavy-handed clap across the back, Shelby tried to get her breath and think of something to say. A.J. didn't even bother to try hiding his fury as he said, "Yes—it would. Do you want the shop, Shelby? I'm sure it would be *perfect* for your business."

Because she had done nothing wrong, Shelby resented the angry glare he was giving her. Even Lynn was looking at him curiously, puzzled by his scathing tone. "I would *love* it," Shelby answered in a contemptuous tone that equaled his.

"Fine. I'll have someone call you about the details." A.J. took Lynn's hand in his and started to lead her away.

Lynn looked from her new fiancé to her old friend. The hostility between them crackled in the air like summer lightning. Shelby saw a question forming in Lynn's eyes.

"You'd better go accept everyone's congratulations," she said brightly, forgetting that she hadn't offered any herself.

Lynn seemed barely to have heard her. She smiled in eager anticipation. "Let's have lunch Monday and begin making plans."

Shelby didn't want to have lunch with Lynn. She wanted to go somewhere and bury her face in her hands, but she smiled shakily at Lynn's eagerness. "Uh...I'll call you."

A.J. didn't even look back as he tucked Lynn's hand into the crook of his elbow and started walking away. "Don't rush into anything, Lynn," he began. "You have no guarantee..."

Shelby frowned. She could almost finish the sentence herself. "No guarantee that La Grande Affaire is any good." Well, she would show him! She groaned inwardly and popped another canapé into her mouth. What was she thinking? She didn't want to make their wedding arrangements! Glancing down she saw the appalling amount of food she had heaped on her plate. She carried it to the kitchen and set it on the nearest counter, then slipped out with a silent apology to Mrs. Moran, who deplored waste.

Back in the patio area she sat down on a lounge chair and watched A.J. and Lynn talking to the society columnist, Anderson. A.J. appeared very solicitous toward Lynn. When she spoke, he gave her his full, smiling attention. His hand was constantly at the back of her waist, or his arm was about her shoulders. The attention he gave her made Shelby think of the way he had treated Erica and Carmen—with affectionate humor and warmth.

But this wasn't Erica or Carmen. This was the woman he was going to marry, she reminded herself. At one point A.J. leaned over and gave Lynn a kiss on the cheek, and Shelby shivered with the memory of what it had been like to kiss him. And then shivered again when she realized the phone call he had received that day at Erica's from his soon-to-be fiancé had also been a phone call from one of her oldest friends.

Watching his handsome face fixed intently on Lynn's as he listened to her, Shelby admitted she was attracted to him. He was everything she wanted, despite her opinion that he was insufferable. He was successful, strong, sensitive—but taken by Lynn, a friend she loved and admired. Shelby shifted uncomfortably. This situation could get very sticky.

One question kept going through her mind. What had happened to Carlo Rosetti? Lynn had been wild about him a few weeks ago. What had gone wrong, and when had A.J. entered the picture? Shelby wished she and Lynn had seen more of each other lately so that the engagement would have been less of a shock.

Brooding wasn't going to help, she knew, so she got up and headed for the bar, where she was handed a glass of wine. She walked toward a group of people she knew and grimly prepared to enjoy herself until she could make her escape. After a while she noticed that Lynn and A.J. had joined separate groups and Lynn danced with several guests.

Half an hour later, Shelby felt that she had stayed long enough and began working her way toward the door. A.J. Court blocked her path before she even got away from the patio area.

"Leaving so soon, Miss Featherstone?"

Although Shelby was tempted, she decided she couldn't very well shove him out of the way in order to leave. "Yes. I promised my mother I wouldn't be out late."

His brow lifted. They both knew she was well past the age when she had to be in by curfew. He shrugged, his wide shoulders moving easily beneath the creamy linen of his jacket. "I understand. After all, why should you stay now that you've accomplished your objective?"

A slow simmering anger began heating up inside her. She placed her hands on her hips and tilted her head as aggressively as he was doing. "My objective?"

"You couldn't convince me any other way, not even by coming to my office or waylaying me on the street, so you ingratiated yourself with Lynn and made your need for a shop known. How did you find out about Lynn? Miss Simmons, again?"

The anger flared into blue sparks in her eyes. "Ingratiated myself, huh? Well, if that's true, I must have been a truly clairvoyant kindergartner."

His eyes narrowed on her. "What do you mean?"

"I mean I've known Lynn Altman since we were five years old."

"Right."

His scoffing tone made her furious. "Didn't you hear Lynn say she had talked to my mother? Certainly that indicated long-term friendship."

"Not necessarily."

Oh, he was so stubborn! Turning on her heel, she started into the house. "Come with me."

He had no alternative but to follow as she swung through the door that led to the main part of the house. At the entrance to Mr. Altman's den she paused and looked back over her shoulder at him. "Perhaps you've never been in this room before...." She allowed her voice to trail off.

"Many times," he growled.

She opened the door and swept inside, certain that the room was just as she remembered. Nothing in the house had been altered since Sanford Altman's sudden death. Mrs. Altman hadn't even been able to reenter the house after the funeral, but had departed for her sister's home down the coast. "Then I'm sure you've seen all these family pictures." Airily, she waved her hand at the walls of the cozy room. "The Altmans were very systematic about these things, especially since Lynn is an only child. Here are Lynn's baby pictures. And here's grade school...." She indicated a photograph of a group of children squinting into the camera. A swing set and a rainbow of monkey bars were in the background.

"This is Lynn." She pointed out a lovely little girl with platinum braids and a pristine dress. "And this—is me." Her finger moved to the next child whose curls were in wild disarray, her blouse pulled out of the waist of her skirt, and her knee sporting a big bandage. "Shortly after a tussle in the sandbox with Billy Muldane." Shelby frowned critically at the photo. "Billy lost."

She chanced a sideways glance at A.J., who was studying the wall solemnly.

"Then of course, there was our sixth-grade play. Lynn played Mary, Queen of Scots. I was one of her guards in the Tower of London." She pointed to a cluster of children in the dress of sixteenth-century England. "My mother made the costumes."

"Moving right along," Shelby continued, her voice taking on the tone of a tour guide. "We see Lynn Altman as homecoming queen, with her handsome king, and Shelby Featherstone as one of her attendants, accompanied by Billy Muldane," she sighed. She was beginning to enjoy herself at A.J.'s expense. "No, no, don't be jealous. The homecoming king is now happily married with a baby on the way. And here—"

"All right, all right. I get the point." A.J. interrupted her monologue. He glanced at the expanse of pictures once again, then at her. His green eyes were dark in thought, his forehead deeply furrowed, as if he was struggling inwardly. "I apologize."

Her heart gave a little jolt of happiness. "Accepted."

They were silent for several minutes while A.J. studied the photographs. He turned to her, an involuntary smile curling up the corner of his mouth. "Whatever happened to Billy Muldane?"

The question was a peace offering, a momentary truce. Shelby's anger faded as quickly as it had flared. She felt drained, tired from the surprises she had received. "He's a professional surfer. He simply never got over that defeat in the sandbox."

A.J.'s lips quirked in a reluctant smile as he nodded and moved away from her to study the other pictures on the walls. Shelby studied him. There were a million questions she wanted to ask. How long had he known Lynn? Didn't the ring fit her finger?

"Who's Marla Gaines?"

His head swung toward her. "What?"

"No, who. Who's Marla Gaines? That lady you were pictured with in the paper."

His smile turned sardonic. "Been looking for me in the papers, hmm?"

Shelby's chin lifted. She shrugged, uncaring. "Creig pointed it out to me. I thought *she* was your fiancée."

Shaking his head, he moved back to her. "Just a lecturer at the museum. I guess she happened to be standing next to me at that charity event when the photographer came around. I don't know her.''

Shelby felt an odd rush of relief. He wasn't engaged to that woman after all. A rush of guilt followed. Instead, he was going to marry Lynn.

If she had known him better or they had just met and had no embarrassing history between them, she would have asked him his feelings for Lynn. Even if she hadn't been raised to speak her mind, her own nature would have prompted her to ask why he was marrying her friend. Love was the obvious answer, wasn't it? He seemed to have a cherishing, protective attitude toward Lynn.

Lynn's physical attributes were probably a big factor. What man wouldn't want to be married to someone so beautiful? Lynn was easygoing, accommodating and quiet. All the things Shelby wasn't.

She couldn't help wondering what might have happened if she and A.J. had met sooner or in different circumstances, but her mind slammed the door on those dangerous thoughts.

He was engaged to marry one of her best friends. She and A.J. would have to be friends, too—for Lynn's sake.

A.J. stopped his circuit of the room and looked at her curiously. ''You were telling the truth.''

''You already apologized.''

He grimaced. ''Considering the way we met and the way you barged into my office, I wouldn't have put it past you to—''

''Don't rub salt in the wound, A.J.,'' she said dryly. ''Besides, wouldn't you have barged in on someone who had turned down your application after promising to take another look at it?''

She had his full attention. He put his hands on his hips and inclined his head in a listening pose. ''What are you talking about? I haven't had time to look at it yet.''

Shelby gaped at him. ''I got another letter, identical to the first one, rejecting my application. You mean that second letter was some kind of mistake?''

The dimple in his left cheek winked at her as he smiled wryly. ''So it appears. I'll look into it. Someone in my office must have mailed you a duplicate rejection.''

''And I barged in on you while you were—''

The dimple deepened. ''Au naturel?''

''I'm sorry.'' She avoided his gaze.

''Next time I'll double-check the lock on the door before I strip.''

His words brought heat to her cheeks. She couldn't keep from looking at him as she remembered what his broad tanned back looked like with water still glistening on it. She remembered, too, how the scent of the soap he had used had rolled toward her on a wave of steam.

As if of its own will, her tongue sneaked out to dampen her suddenly dry lips. He was watching her with a very masculine awareness in his green eyes.

Talking about such things was a mistake. They both seemed to realize it at the same time. She swung away from him and headed for the door. The party was over as far as she was concerned.

''Oh, Shelby.''

Reluctantly, she turned back, her hand on the doorknob. ''Yes?''

He stared at her for a moment. His eyes were as dark green as the Pacific before a storm. His face worked as if he was wrestling with many emotions. She saw suspicion, curiosity and dismay. His eyes narrowed, shutting off the emotions she had seen. When he spoke, she knew suspicion had won.

"I still think it's more than coincidence that you were here tonight."

So much for their truce. She was disappointed at how quickly his suspicions had returned. "You know, I read somewhere that everyone knows at least a thousand people well enough to greet them by name," she said, seething. "Santa Barbara is a large city but not so large that we might never have met. Coincidences happen a lot more often than you think," she said, with an ache of regret.

THE RESTAURANT SALAD BAR looked sadly depleted when Shelby and Lynn finished and carried their loaded plates to their table.

When Lynn had called the day after her party and asked her to lunch the next day, Shelby had stalled. Lynn had sounded so hurt that Shelby had finally agreed to come. They had met at Alfy's, their favorite place for salad.

"I've been eating like a pig lately," Lynn sighed, slipping into her chair and picking up her fork.

With a resigned sigh, Shelby observed her friend's slim figure. Lynn was wearing a white eyelet blouse with a wide lace collar and a green suede skirt that emphasized her tiny waist. "Well, if you have, it doesn't show. I think every extra calorie you eat has been showing up on my hips."

Lynn smiled her sweet, serene smile. "You look wonderful, as always."

How could she be jealous of Lynn, Shelby wondered. She was completely guileless. "You're probably overeating because you're happy and content." Shelby wished she could say the same for herself. Her food binges were brought on for just the opposite reasons.

Lynn's fork, trailing alfalfa sprouts and carrot curls, paused halfway to her mouth. She blinked in surprise. "I guess so," she said, then chewed thoughtfully for a moment. "I hadn't thought about it."

She put down her fork and leaned forward eagerly. "We'd better start making plans. I know it's going to take a long time to do everything." Lynn propped her chin on her palm and smiled dreamily. "I want it all to be perfect."

"Well, what is the date? This winter?" Shelby wished they were talking about anything but the wedding.

"I haven't decided yet."

"*You* haven't?" Shelby stared at her. "Doesn't A.J. have any say in this?"

Lynn blinked, coming out of her rosy fog. "Who?"

Color washed up Shelby's cheeks. "A.J. Court. I call him that. Seems to me it fits him better."

Speculative brown eyes took in her embarrassment. "Oh, yes. I heard you call Alex that at the party. Maybe it does fit him better." She was quiet for a moment, then said, "I have free rein on the wedding plans. After all, I'm paying for it."

Shelby was speechless at the strangeness of that remark. In these days of two-career couples, she had discovered that most brides and grooms paid for their own weddings. Very seldom any more did the bride and her family have to carry the full expense. "You mean your mother will be paying for it."

"No," Lynn said firmly, her face taking on a determination Shelby had never seen in Lynn before. "Mother won't be involved until the last minute. She still hasn't recovered from Dad's death, you know. I can't expect her to come back here and help me just yet." Lynn busied herself with buttering a roll.

"Oh, of course," Shelby agreed. Slowly she resumed eating. She could understand Lynn's reasoning, but the Altmans had always doted on their daughter, almost to the point of smothering her. Maybe Lynn just felt she needed to do this on her own.

"So," Lynn said brightly. "When can I talk to your mom and Lindy about my wedding gown?"

"Oh, Lynn...." Shelby looked at her friend in dismay. She knew it was a bad idea to take on the job, considering her ridiculous attraction to A.J.—and his distrust of her. "I don't know."

"Why? What's the matter?" Lynn asked, worried.

Shelby shook her head. "Things just aren't... worked out yet...the shop and all."

As Lynn's eyes searched her face, Shelby felt herself turning red.

"I thought you and Alex were working out the details about the shop."

"We are. Someone from his office called this morning. I'm to tour the property and sign the lease." Despite her misery over Lynn's plans, Shelby couldn't hide the excited pride in her voice.

"Well, then, what's the problem?"

"It's going to take a while to get the place organized."

Lynn fluttered her fingers airily. "Don't worry. I'm not in that much of a hurry." She smiled suddenly, slyly. "It's going to take me a while to get organized, too. Besides, you of all people know what kind of wedding I want. We talked about it often enough as little girls."

Shelby nodded and took a sip of iced tea to give herself a moment to think. Of course she remembered. Lynn was deeply romantic, even more so than Shelby.

Lynn wanted her wedding picture-perfect with no expense spared. As a professional, Shelby saw it as an incredibly exciting challenge. As Lynn's friend—the traitor attracted to her fiancé—Shelby saw it as a potential nightmare of guilt and remorse.

Lynn watched the play of emotions on Shelby's face. She straightened her back suddenly and looked away, pain forming in the depths of her velvety brown eyes. "Unless you don't *want* to do my wedding," she said in a low voice aching with hurt. "Tell me, Shelby. Have I done something wrong? Hurt you somehow?"

Shelby's hand shot across the table to cover Lynn's. "No, of course not," she said sincerely, aware that *she* was the one who had done something wrong. She had done it unknowingly, but she didn't want to compound the mistake. Seeing the hurt in Lynn's face Shelby knew what her decision had to be. She simply couldn't hurt her friend. She would take on Lynn's wedding—and stay away from the groom, thus avoiding a greater hurt. That should be easy enough, she thought wryly, since he seemed to dislike her so. "I'll do your wedding, Lynn," she said gently. "Everything will be just as you want it."

Thrilled and relieved, Lynn covered Shelby's hand with her own and squeezed. "Thanks. This means so much to me." Lynn's eyes took on a delightfully wistful expression. She looked like a woman in love.

"Where did you meet him?" Shelby asked suddenly.

Lynn started, her eyes snapping to Shelby. "You mean Alex?"

Shelby shook her head in puzzlement. She had never seen Lynn so dreamy. "Yes, your fiancé—remember him...?"

"He was one of Dad's protegeés. Dad helped Alex get started in business, and they were partners in several investments. I'm sure you've heard me talk about him. He's been over to the house. In fact, I can't believe you two hadn't met there before."

Shelby thought back. She vaguely recalled Lynn mentioning her father's friend Alex, but she had assumed he was a contemporary of Mr. Altman's.

"He's been such a help this past year," Lynn continued. "He's very good to me."

Shelby had no doubt of that. People were always good to Lynn. "I'm sure he is," she murmured.

"He helped out with the lawyers... probate... everything. He came to San Diego with papers to sign because Mother wouldn't come back here. We can trust him." Lynn chewed slowly on another bite of salad. "I can depend on him. I feel safe with him," she concluded.

Safe? Shelby nearly choked on a crouton. Safe with the thorough masculinity that was so much a part of him? Safe with his keen mind and quick wit? Safe with the hard-driving businessman who could be such a dangerous adversary? Her own feelings were exactly the opposite. She found him exciting and disconcert-ing, not dependable and friendly.

Lynn held up her left hand. "He brought the ring over yesterday," she said, watching the light wink in the stone. "He was having it enlarged. I don't know how he knew it would be too small."

Shelby did. Under the table, she folded her hand so her thumb could rub over the place that had been chafed by the ring he'd intended for Lynn. She won-dered if A.J. ever planned to tell Lynn what had hap-pened with her ring. If he didn't, Erica or Carmen might. They obviously adored him, but she didn't think they would pass up the opportunity to tease him about the incident. Lynn would probably think it was pretty minor, anyway. She had a good sense of hu-mor. But if that minor happening could be dismissed so easily, Shelby knew there was something—some-one—in Lynn's past that might not be so easily dis-missed.

"Lynn, I haven't asked before, and you can tell me to mind my own business if you want, but what hap-pened to Carlo Rosetti?"

Carefully avoiding Shelby's eyes, Lynn laid down her fork and pushed her plate away. "Carlo? Why do you ask?"

Shelby watched as Lynn's fingers stiffened at the edge of her plate. "Curiosity. Weren't you in love with him less than two months ago?"

"He's not ready to settle down."

"And you are."

"Yes." Lynn's voice was very low. "Racing is his life." She looked up, her eyes lively. "It's very excit-ing. Watching him race was wonderful—but frightening. My heart was in my mouth the whole time. Not knowing if he would win or lose or—"

Shelby nodded, encouraging her to keep talking.

The animation faded from Lynn's features, replaced by an unusual gleam. "My parents didn't approve of him, and he thinks I've got too much money. He's from a very poor family," she added.

Shelby nodded. "I can see where that would cause problems."

"It didn't have to," Lynn said fiercely. "We could have overcome it. If he'd been willing to compromise and make a commitment." One slim hand balled into a fist. "He just won't make a commitment."

"And A.J. will?"

Lynn blinked. "Oh, yes, Alex would."

If she didn't know Lynn so well, she would think she was marrying A.J. because she couldn't have the one she really wanted. Shelby didn't think Lynn would set A.J. up for that kind of hurt. Everything she had said about him bespoke deep affection and caring.

Lynn sounded reasonable, and she didn't give of herself easily. She must care very much for him, Shelby decided. Wanting reassurance, she touched her friend's hand. "You do love him, don't you?"

Lynn looked her right in the eye, her expression wildly earnest. "Absolutely," she said.

CHAPTER FIVE

"I THINK IT NEEDS to be a little farther to the left." Shelby blew her bangs off her forehead and leaned against the storeroom door. She watched as her father and brother-in-law attempted to position a full-length mirror against the back wall of the fitting room.

"No, to the right." From his position on the floor—back propped against the wall, legs spread in front of him, hands behind his head—Creig offered his opinion.

"If you know so much about it, why don't you get up and help?" Shelby asked crossly, wiping her damp brow and pulling her loose T-shirt away from her perspiring back.

The fitting room had been painted a pale mauve and papered in a hazily striped paper of mauve and blue. Only the finishing touches were left. It wouldn't take long to hang a couple of potted plants and fit the swinging doors.

"Hey, Shel, I'm supervising," Creig said. An exasperated look from his mother, who was scrubbing down the walls and woodwork of the main room in preparation for painting, had him getting to his feet and lifting one corner of the mirror. With the three of them working, they soon had it fitted into its brackets.

Shelby looked around at the shop. Her mother and all three of her sisters had come along to help. The amount of help Lindy and Charmaine had been able to give was severely limited, though, by the presence of their offspring. Lindy's son, Nathan, and Charmaine's daughter, Becky, were four and two. In the past hour Nathan had painted the front of his father's jeans, and Becky had fallen into the bucket of sudsy water the women were using for scrubbing. In desperation Charmaine had tied one end of a piece of drapery cord to the back of Becky's rompers. The other end was attached to the leg of an old sofa that the last tenants had abandoned in the shop. Even though Becky could roam the length of the six-foot cord without getting hurt and she had several toys to play with, her limited freedom frustrated her. The adults took turns sitting down for a few minutes to play with her. Of course, Creig's turn had stretched out twice as long as anyone else's.

As promised, the assistant manager of Court Properties had given Shelby the keys on Monday. The family had spent all week helping her fix up the shop. Shelby and Charmaine had put their heads together and come up with an interior design that was both chic and inviting. The color scheme was blue and mauve with generous touches of navy carefully added to make the male visitors feel comfortable. Two plush chairs would face the desk she had lovingly refinished in a golden oak stain. A navy-blue sofa would face a low table in a conversation group.

Charmaine had found a bargain on two Stiffel lamps and an oriental rug. Even with a decorator's discount for the furnishings, though, all the remodeling had put a big dent in the money Shelby had inherited from her great aunt.

With careful planning and enough word-of-mouth advertising, she would be able to pay all of her bills and the rent on time. She was determined that A. J. Court would not have to wait for his money. Unfortunately that meant the shop's back room couldn't yet be converted into a sewing room for Mary and Lindy. Finished gowns could be kept there, but the sewing would still have to be done at home.

"Shelby, have you decided what kind of sign you're going to have outside?" Mary asked, pausing in her work.

The family thought the interior design was great, but when it came to discussions about a tasteful but eyecatching theme for the outside, everyone had a different opinion.

Shelby shook her head. "I don't know."

Sienna dropped her cleaning rag back into the bucket and stood. She put her hand behind her and massaged the small of her back. The most petite of the Featherstone women, Sienna was also the prettiest, with big doe eyes of deep gray fringed by incredibly thick lashes. She had been looking tired lately and Shelby had been reluctant to let her help, but Sienna had insisted. Her husband, Ray, had promised to pick her up early on his way home from work.

"I think you should carry out the same color scheme," Sienna said.

"Not necessarily," Mary added with a wistful smile. "You need to build a flower box and spell out the name of the shop in pansies."

"I know a guy who does great hand-lettered signs," Lindy's husband, Mark, said, bending down to recover his screwdriver from his son's back pocket. "He could have one ready in no time. Fancy lettering, the whole bit."

Here we go again, Shelby thought in amusement, preparing to referee the discussion.

"Don't be a dwede, Mark," Creig said, taking the opportunity of everyone's distraction to lean against the freshly papered wall. "It needs to be in neon. Neon's in right now."

Belligerently, Lindy put her hands on her hips. "Oh that's just what this shop needs—high-tech tack."

"Creig, I'm afraid they're right. The style has to be consistent with the rest of the mall. It was in the agreement Shelby signed. Neon wouldn't fit."

At the sound of a new voice, the family swung their heads toward the door.

A. J. Court stood in the entrance, looking over the shop's interior with interest.

Shelby felt a ridiculous surge of gladness. She knew he was probably there to find fault but, oh, he looked good in his neat pin-striped blue suit, gray shirt and tie.

She lifted her chin. There was nothing for him to find fault with, anyway. She and Charmaine had studied the decor in every other store in the mall and they had come up with a design consistent with them. "Good afternoon, Mr. Court."

The amused look he gave her threw her completely off balance. "Hi, Shelby."

His gaze ranged around the shop, lighting on the new fitting rooms with their pretty paint and paper.

"Nice," he said.

Shelby's jaw dropped. Hadn't they left each other, daggers drawn, just a few days ago? He had been thinking the worst of her.

"Come in, Mr. Court," Mary invited. "As you can see, the family is helping Shelby get things ready."

A.J. nodded and smiled warmly at the assembled group. Shelby eyed him warily while her family cheerfully introduced themselves and shook hands. Even Nathan solemnly put his small hand in the stranger's and asked if he wanted to see a hammer. When A.J. agreed, the little boy produced the tool he had filched from his father and hidden under a cushion on the couch.

Amid the laughter A.J. admired it while Nathan beamed.

"Won't you sit down?" Mary asked, indicating the worn sofa where little Becky was imprisoned. "The sofa isn't really diseased, it just looks that way."

"I know," he said, flashing a smile at her assembled family. "The last tenants left it here. I think they hauled it in for spite. It wasn't in the shop while they were here selling lingerie."

Shelby wondered if he had spent much time inspecting the merchandise of the former establishment. Behind his back Shelby's three sisters exchanged looks. "Who is he?" Lindy mouthed. "The landlord?"

Shelby nodded, gesturing to encompass the room.

Lindy's blue eyes widened. "Lynn's fiancé?"

Nodding again, Shelby glanced around to see A.J. watching her curiously. She plastered a smile onto her face. "Have a seat," she chirped.

When he had seated himself, Becky climbed up beside him and began flirting madly in hopes that the newcomer would untie her from the cord attached to her rompers.

To Shelby's amazement, he picked up the toddler and plopped her onto his lap. Surveying her bonds, he said, "Hey, you must be a dangerous character to be tied up like this." Becky lifted melting brown eyes to him and smiled. A.J. ran a finger down her velvety cheek.

"Watch her," Charmaine warned. "She's a direct descendent of Mae West. Never met a man she didn't like."

A.J. chuckled and allowed the little girl to pull his precisely folded gray silk handkerchief from his pocket and begin playing peekaboo with it.

"Shelby, we were right about that second notice you got," A.J. said, leaning back and settling Becky against him more comfortably. "One of my assistants sent you a duplicate before I had time to review your application."

Shelby shrugged and smoothed the hem of her old T-shirt down over her shorts. She wasn't sure how to take this friendly, relaxed side of him because she didn't know the reason behind it. "It's all right," she said cautiously. "Everything has worked out."

Becky had discovered A.J.'s heavy gold tie clip. Blithely, he unclipped it and let her play with it.

Shelby glanced at the baby, who was playing with what must have been a piece of solid gold jewelry, and back at A.J. Over the little girl's downy head, his eyes met hers. He smiled, a warm, full-blown smile that caused a kick of awareness in Shelby's stomach.

Amazing, she thought, letting her eyes feast on him. He tricked sweet old ladies into giving up cigarettes and entertained baby girls. Females of all ages fell at his feet like ripe peaches, including her—and Lynn.

Remembering her friend helped bring Shelby out of the daydream. She whipped her eyes from his and glanced around at her family. Her sisters were watching her in amusement, her parents in alarm.

"The shop looks good, Shelby," he complimented. "The color scheme has class."

He couldn't have said anything that would have pleased her family more.

Joe and Mary looked frankly astounded. Shelby imagined they were wondering if this could be the same grim-faced stranger who had been in their kitchen a couple of weeks ago.

"Thank you," she stammered. "We'll be finished in a week. Our only problem is a sign for the outside."

"I've been thinking about that," he said. "I was wondering if you might consider a name change."

"A name change?" Shelby repeated in a carefully neutral tone. Here it comes, she thought. The real reason for the folksy visit. She was tempted to go pluck her niece from his lap.

"You look skeptical," he said with a wry twist to his lips. "Wait until you've heard what it is."

"I'm listening."

He paused a moment for effect. Not that he needed it. Everyone in the room was waiting breathlessly.

He really should have been an actor, she thought, remembering their lunch at Erica's. He knew how to hold an audience.

"Since your last name is so unusual and your business will basically be run by the women in your family—" He glanced around at the sweaty, disarranged females. Automatically, they each straightened their clothes or smoothed their hair. "Why don't you call the shop Featherstone Brides?"

There was a moment of silence while the family mulled over his suggestion, then smiles broke out all around.

"That's a wonderful idea," Mary twittered. "Why didn't we think of that?"

Shelby looked around at her family. They were all so delighted with the idea she knew she would have gone along with it even if she hadn't liked it so much herself. Even Joe, Mark and Creig seemed impressed. "That *is* a wonderful idea," she said, smiling down at him.

A.J.'s green eyes held a mysterious glow as if he saw something that pleased him. A familiar heating started in her pulses.

It was disconcerting that he had such an effect on her. Nothing like it had ever happened to her before. She was aware of him on a level deeper than any she had ever known. As she watched him, a feminine longing on her face, his smile deepened and his lopsided dimple pocked the corner of his mouth engagingly. She had an overwhelming desire to put her little finger there. She lifted her hand.

Her dad cleared his throat loudly. "Well, if you'll excuse us, Mr. Court, we've got to get back to work. Mark and Creig, why don't you finish with that door? I'll start painting the main room."

Dazed, Shelby looked around. Her father was staring at her, his eyes narrowed beneath his bushy brows. She turned to find something—anything—to do.

"I'll be going," A.J. said, setting Becky aside with a look of regret.

"You're welcome to stay," Shelby said quickly. "If you don't mind the noise."

"I don't mind," he answered, settling back beside Becky who had begun wailing. "I'd offer to help, but I have to admit, I'm all thumbs with a hammer or paint roller."

"That's okay," Charmaine and Lindy said almost in unison, exchanging looks of relief. "You can baby-sit."

Joe picked up his paint roller and began rolling it carefully in a tray full of pale blue paint. "You know, nothing good gets accomplished unless there's a noise involved," he said, in a thoughtful voice.

"I don't think that's necessarily true of *everything* good. Trees grow, nature changes, and they don't make noise," Mary said, following behind him with a damp rag to wipe up paint specks.

"We just don't *hear* it," Joe argued.

The four sisters exchanged amused glances. A.J., running a small car up Becky's chubby leg, had a confused expression on his face. *Get used to it,* Shelby thought. *You haven't seen anything yet.*

Indeed, during the next half hour A.J. listened, seemingly amazed, as her parents continued their discussion. Everyone else went on with their work except Sienna, who joined A.J. on the couch. She helped play with Becky and Nathan until her husband, Ray, strolled through the door with a video camera held high. Sienna hopped up with a glad smile that he captured on tape.

"All right, everybody," he said, panning the camera slowly around the room. "We're here to record for posterity the completion of Shelby's shop. Everybody line up."

"Line up?" they chorused. "That's not the way to film something."

"It's the way *I* film," Ray said, exchanging a sparkling glance with his wife.

"Please everybody, humor us," Sienna pleaded, shepherding her family in front of the freshly painted wall.

A.J. leaned back comfortably and spread his arms along the back of the sofa as he enjoyed the milling about that finally sorted itself into a lineup of the Featherstone clan.

"Hurry up, Ray," Creig said, looping his arm around Shelby's neck and leaning on her. "We've got work to do."

This brought loud hoots of derision from his family.

"Keep your shirt on, Creig," Ray said. "I want us to look back on this, when there's a string of Shelby's shops across the country, and remember what we all looked like on this day."

Involuntarily, Shelby's eyes went to A.J. who grinned at her. Shops all across the country, she thought. How about that?

"Also," Ray continued. "I wanted to tell you that Sienna has been to the doctor a couple of times lately."

The family exchanged concerned glances, which were duly recorded on the tape. Mary reached out and put her arm around Sienna, who smiled slyly.

Ray went on. "And Sienna and I want to always remember what you looked like when we told you we're going to have a baby."

The family broke apart and everyone rushed toward Sienna at once. Laughing, she accepted their congratulations. Creig confiscated the camera from

Ray and continued taping while his brother-in-law received warm handshakes and hearty backslaps.

Peeking around the melee of relatives Shelby saw that A.J. had risen from the couch. In the crush of people she found herself pushed with him to the back of the room. "We're not usually like this," she said, stepping out of the way of her father who was unabashedly sniffling into a handkerchief.

"Oh, well, I've enjoyed—" A.J. began, sounding somewhat bemused as Creig wobbled the video camera in front of his face.

"We're usually worse," Shelby finished, her eyes twinkling. "The Featherstone clan tends to be loud, emotional and—"

"Procreative?" he supplied, as Becky scampered behind her aunt and wound the piece of drapery cord around Shelby's legs.

Shelby stumbled against A.J., whose hands shot out to grab her waist. He lost his balance, and the two of them tumbled back onto the sofa. Creig kept right on taping as the two of them tried to extricate themselves from the cord and the little girl who had been dragged backward with them.

Half on top of A.J. Shelby tried to push herself up and rescue Becky at the same time. "I think it's time to untie this kid before she strangles someone," she gasped, trying to ignore the hard male body beneath her.

He wasn't helping at all. His sharply handsome features looked boyishly delighted at her predicament. Instead of helping her disentangle her legs, he leaned back a little farther so that she was fully on top of him.

Her legs were bound together at the knees, and Becky was plastered up against her right hip. Instead of trying to free them, A.J. put his hand in the small of Shelby's back, making her fully aware of him. His other hand supported Becky.

"Hey, little one," he said to Becky. "You've caused quite a problem here."

"I'm sorry," Shelby gasped, her face flaming. "I've got to get—off. We're squashing you."

A.J. was laughing at her, his green eyes dark with humor. Finally he removed his warm hand from her back. "Oh, don't hurry. I'm beginning to think this kind of thing is normal in your family."

She gave him a repressive look, but its thunder was stolen by the blush on her cheeks. Knowing she had to get away from him, she finally managed to scramble up and untie Becky who had chortled throughout the entire episode. Her face down, Shelby talked in a rapid, breathless tone. "These must be the strongest buttons in the world. They should have broken off." A few flicks of her wrist had the knots in the cord untied and the romper straps straightened and rebuttoned. Becky toddled away, and Shelby was working up her courage to face A.J. when the phone rang.

"I'll get it," she called, leaping forward.

"Hey, all right," Creig said enthusiastically, following her like a bloodhound on the trail, the camera whirring away. "The first call on your new business phone."

Shelby turned her back on him. "Hello?"

Too late, she remembered she should have used her new business name. Thinking of it, Featherstone Brides, gave her a surge of pleasure.

"Shelby, is that you?"

"Hello, Lynn? Yes, it's me."

"Is Alex there? He said he was going to stop by your shop this afternoon." Lynn's voice sounded hurried, excited.

"Yes—yes, he is." Shelby turned and waved the phone at him. "It's Lynn," she called over the din. Into the receiver, she said, "You sound like you've been running."

Lynn laughed. "Not yet."

Shelby frowned at the receiver. Lynn was acting very odd lately, nervous and high-strung—like a woman in love, she concluded.

He took the receiver and clapped a hand over his exposed ear. Shelby shushed her family as they began to clean up and gather their tools and belongings in preparation for going home.

"You did what!" A.J.'s voice sounded over the noise in the room. Several heads swung toward him. He smiled quickly, turned his back on them and continued talking, keeping his voice low. "The Los Angeles paper? Do you really think that's a good—"

Shelby moved away before she heard any more of the conversation, which had sounded like a lovers' quarrel. She felt unreasonably disheartened at the thought of Lynn and A.J. being lovers. Of course they were. They were engaged.

Shelby frisked Nathan for more of Mark's tools and, finding a couple of nails in his back pocket, returned them to Mark's tool chest. She came back just in time to rescue a toy giraffe from extinction at the hands of her niece and nephew, and stuffed it into the big canvas tote bag Charmaine had brought along.

"I hope everything's okay, Mr. Court," she heard her mother say.

Shelby turned. A.J. was standing directly behind her, watching her with narrowed eyes. Nervously she stepped back and dropped the toy bag beside Becky's diaper bag. A.J.'s face cleared, and once again he was the pleasant guest.

He lingered, chatting with Joe and Mark until the family had all said goodbye and drifted away.

When they were alone A.J. turned to Shelby. "I'd better be going, too."

Shelby smiled. "Thank you for coming by, and for suggesting the new name."

He nodded, giving the room one last look. His hand was reaching for the doorknob when he turned back. "I had a dinner date scheduled, but it looks like I've been stood up again." He gave her an abashed grin. "I hate to eat alone. Would you join me for dinner?"

"Oh, I don't know...." she hedged, unable to think of a single good reason not to but sure she shouldn't.

"Don't tell me," he said, with a mock frown. "You've got to get home and fix dinner for your husband and six kids."

"Seven, but who's counting?"

"Or—you've got a date with an irresistible man."

"Not me," she grinned, spreading her hands to plead her innocence. *He* was irresistible, and despite her better judgment, she had never been the type to resist what impulse told her to do. But he was Lynn's fiancé, an inner voice reminded her, and Lynn was her friend. It certainly couldn't be called a *date*, though, she rationalized. And she really should get to know him.

"Well, will you have dinner with me?"

She glanced down at her shorts and baggy T-shirt. "I'm not exactly dressed for—"

"Nothing fancy," he said quickly. "We can go to McDonald's. I haven't eaten there in years."

"Well..." To her mortification, her stomach growled.

A.J.'s face grew very solemn. "Either you ate a tiger for lunch or you're hungry."

"A gentleman wouldn't mention such a thing," she said huffily.

"A lady would accept a gentleman's invitation to dinner."

Shelby smiled and nodded.

"THE LAST FRENCH FRY," A.J. said lazily, waving it near her mouth.

Shelby shook her head. "I'm full."

"Quite an admission—for you."

"Now don't you start," she said placidly, pushing away from the rock where she was sitting. "I get enough of that from Creig."

They had bought a couple of Big Macs and some fries and driven to the beach. At this time of day in the late summer, the area was almost deserted.

Shelby had left her shoes in A.J.'s car and persuaded him to do the same. He had been reluctant, but she was very convincing, even talking him into shedding his coat and tie and rolling up the legs of his slacks. He complained that he looked ridiculous. Privately, Shelby thought he looked casual and sexy. They had perched on the top of a group of rocks to eat.

"I like watching you eat...." He paused, crumpling up the white paper carryout bag. "You enjoy things."

"I do enjoy food," she sighed, mentally adding up the calories she had just consumed.

They wandered to the nearest trash can and chucked in their garbage. Shelby kept walking, following a set of sandpiper tracks stitched into the wet sand.

It was wonderful to think of all they had done at the shop that day. She liked the feeling of being pleasantly tired and spending time with someone fascinating. She was eager to get to know him, and justified her interest by thinking she could use her knowledge of him to better plan his wedding to Lynn.

Turning, she followed the tracks back to his side.

A.J. had stuck his hands in his pockets, and stood gazing out in the direction of the Channel Islands. It was almost dark and the sun sent its last rays slanting across the water. The red-gold half-light softened his brooding features, making him seem more approachable. The wind ruffled his black hair, and he settled it back into place with his fingers. Shelby walked up beside him and matched his stance, hands in pockets, gazing at the hypnotic surf.

"What are you thinking about?" she asked on impulse.

He didn't answer at first, but his slow smile sent warmth sifting through her.

"That your family is different than I would have expected."

"Different?" she asked cautiously. "You mean flaky."

He winced as she turned his own words of days ago back on him. "No," he said looking at her intently. "Supportive, like you said."

"Hmm," she said noncommittally, beginning to walk slowly down the beach again. She noticed a few other strollers out enjoying the autumn warmth.

A.J. fell into step beside her. "Your names are all a bit unusual, except for Lindy."

"It's short for Melisande."

"I should have guessed."

She smiled, appreciating his humored acceptance. "Mom's maiden name was Jones...Mary Jones. She figured we all needed something pretty remarkable to go with Featherstone."

A.J. tilted his head as he looked down at her, his gaze lingering on her disheveled appearance. "Your parents are remarkable."

Self-consciously, she smoothed her wind-tossed curls. "Believe me, you haven't seen anything yet." She laughed suddenly, rolling her eyes heavenward and shaking her head. "You should have seen them when Lindy became old enough to date. Dad used to have long, philosophical discussions with her dates on everything from world hunger to metaphysics. Lindy would be standing around, all dressed up, shifting from one foot to the other. Unfortunately most of her dates weren't very tolerant of Dad's quirks—until Mark came along."

"What did he do differently?"

"Listened."

A.J. raised his chin in a gesture of understanding humor.

Shelby stopped at the edge of the waves. The cold Pacific washed up to her toes then slid back on itself. A.J. didn't speak for a long time. Finally, his eyes on the surf, he said, "My mother was quiet, and my dad was even quieter. They worked themselves to early graves."

Shelby stood very still, sensing that such an admission was very difficult for him. "What did they do for a living?"

"They were farmers." He paused then shook his head as if he was having trouble saying what was on his mind. "They were migrant workers until I was thirteen."

Shelby's eyes widened. "I've never met anyone before who..."

A.J.'s chin thrust out again—this time defensively. His glance sliced down at her. "Picked other people's crops for a living?"

"Yes." She shrugged. "You've come a long way," she said, looking at his perfectly tailored slacks rolled up around his hairy, muscular calves.

Suddenly he pulled his hands from his pockets and held them up. Examining the palms, he said. "You'll never know how far. Mom and Dad bought a little farm in Ventura County when I was in high school. I was drafted and spent three years in the army. They both died before I got out."

Shelby sank onto the sand, her blue eyes never leaving him, silently inviting him to join her. He hesitated, looking into her eyes for a long moment before he sat down, lifting his knees to rest his elbows on them and clasping his hands loosely. Shelby had to watch carefully to read his changing expressions.

She couldn't imagine what it must have been like as a boy fresh out of high school to leave his family, go off to war and come home to find everything changed. Erica and her family may have represented the only stability left in his life.

"So you came home to nothing."

He turned his head, resting his chin on his muscled arm. The pose made him seem vulnerable and pensive. "Not exactly. I came home to the Southern California real estate boom. I never wanted to pick another crop and I couldn't bear to live at home with my parents gone," he said fervently. "So I sold the farm. It's now a five-hundred-home development."

"What did you do then?"

"What do you think? Twenty-one years old with more money than I'd ever seen before. I bought a Corvette."

Shelby threw back her head and laughed. "Every boy's dream."

A.J. ran his thumb along his cheek where five-o'clock shadow was beginning to show. "I was pretty wild," he admitted. "More money than sense, I guess. I met Sanford Altman by chance—"

Shelby detected a wry note in his voice. "By chance?"

"I hit his car one night when he and Sharon were driving home. I had been drinking." When Shelby gasped, he added, "I was the only one hurt."

"You were injured?" Shelby asked, appalled at the thought of him being in pain.

"Not in the fender bender we had, but Sanford packed a hell of a right punch!" He rubbed his jaw as if he could still feel the connection.

Shelby fell back on the sand as she laughed, picturing short, pudgy Mr. Altman "duking it out" with A.J. "Did you feel as if you'd been attacked by Santa Claus?"

"How did you guess? Anyway, when we got to know each other, he made me realize I was wasting more than money, so I went back to school. He started me in business, too. He was my mentor and friend,'' he said in tones of deep affection and respect.

Listening, Shelby smiled. She had really liked Mr. Altman. He'd treated her kindly, as he had every girl who'd had the good sense to be his daughter's friend.

She lay in an abandoned sprawl, wearing dirty clothes and bare feet. Her short brown curls held paint specks and now sand, and her big blue eyes were soft with pleasant memories. A.J. grinned back at her, then his smile faded. His look became intent. Slowly, as if afraid she would bolt, he reached out and touched a silky brown strand of hair. Shelby froze, staring up at him. He looked faintly puzzled for a moment. He seemed to have forgotten what he was saying.

Very carefully he arranged each of her curls against the sand as though he was a photographer about to immortalize her on film. Shelby didn't move—barely breathed. Her heart was pounding in her ears, sending blood in a mad rush through her. His touch was as gentle as a breeze, his face as intent as that of someone searching for gold. He lowered himself onto one elbow beside her until his face was only inches from hers. His mouth smiled, but his eyes were unreadable.

His palm found her cheek, the pad of his thumb journeying across her cheekbone and up to the corner of her eye. Shelby's eyelids trembled shut. His touch seemed to burn while comforting her at the same time. Amazing how so simple an action could bring her to such an intense state of longing. All thought suspended, she waited in an agony of anticipation for whatever would happen next.

"If you want to pull out of the arrangements for this wedding, I'll be glad to pay whatever fee you ask," he said quietly.

It took several seconds for his words to soak into her befuddled brain. Her eyes snapped open. "What?" she breathed, blinking in astonishment.

"Tell Lynn whatever you want—the shop isn't ready yet, you've got too many clients, your sister's having a baby—I don't care—just pull out." He sat back on one knee, watching her face.

The sensual fog he had created around her was clearing as fast as mist before the sun. She sat bolt upright, her eyes snapping furiously. "I can't pull out, unless it's what Lynn wants, and I know she doesn't."

"Shelby," he said with great patience, apparently oblivious to her anger. "This wedding isn't what you think."

She scrambled to her feet and clapped her hands onto her hips. Belligerently, she glared at him. "Isn't what I think? It's two people saying their vows before their assembled friends and family, isn't it?"

He stood up beside her, his long sinewy body making it seem like one easy motion. "Not exactly."

"Do you want to be married skydiving from an airplane? Or scuba diving underwater? I can arrange that."

"No," he said, shaking his head and frowning down at her.

She pointed an accusatory finger at him. "You don't think I know what I'm doing. You feel coerced into renting me that shop. You think I'm going to fall on my face and take your wedding plans down with me."

His eyes were sparkling now with a familiar angry light. "Believe it or not, Shelby, I really don't doubt your abilities," he said, folding his arms across his chest. "I'm doing this for your own good!"

She threw her head back. "Ha! I *don't* believe it. This whole friendly routine has been building up to this. Meeting my family, telling me about yours..." She paused, doubting the truth of that. It didn't seem as though it had been easy for him to talk about his family. She didn't know if she was more furious with him or herself. She had been acting like a fool, forgetting how single-minded he could be and falling into a stupid daydream. She didn't know what was happening to her. He was going to marry her friend but when she was near him, she kept forgetting that.

"Coming up with a new name for your shop—a better one," he said, adding to her fury.

And if only it wasn't so darned perfect she wouldn't use it, she thought.

She took a calming breath, trying to think rationally. "If you're going to make some kind of decision about your wedding plans I think Lynn had better be in on it."

"As far as she's concerned, the decision is made," A.J. answered grimly.

"Then there's nothing further to discuss. If you're not happy with my work, you can dismiss me. But at least *see* my work."

A.J. lifted his hands in a gesture of defeat. "I tried," he said. "Don't blame me if this doesn't turn out as you expect."

Shelby stared at him.

"You know, Shelby," he went on, "you're just as persistent as I thought you were the day we met."

"And you're just as bullheaded," she snapped. "I don't know what Lynn sees in you!"

Immediately she knew she had gone too far. She tried to back away, but he stepped close and took her arm. He drew her forward, his warm hand sending shivers over her flesh. A.J. put his face close to hers and she stared at him, her eyes huge. Although dark was closing in fast, she could see his face clearly. Sensual awareness arced between them like an electric shock. His knowing look told her that he knew she felt it.

His voice was low when he spoke, as rich as dark chocolate but earthy and warm. "Oh, you don't, do you?"

CHAPTER SIX

"FEATHERSTONE BRIDES," Shelby whispered, looking at the new sign above her shop door. The name A.J. had coined was painted on a pristine white board carved in the shape of a wedding guest register. The letters were handwritten in feathery strokes of blue, ending in a quill pen. The sign looked as if someone had just finished writing and left the pen in place.

Delighted, Shelby shut the door. This was the second week her shop had been open, and at least the hundredth time she had opened the door to look at the new sign. The other mall personnel probably thought she was crazy, but she couldn't help it. The dream she'd had for years had come true. All her hard work had finally paid off.

She would have spun in a joyful dance around the room if the picture window hadn't been in full view of the mall, and if she hadn't been trying to project a businesslike image. Even her clothing had been carefully chosen to display just the right degree of romanticism mixed with professionalism. After careful discussion with her mother and Lindy, she had begun wearing the most feminine and appealing of her clothes. Today she had on a pastel pink skirt with a matching blouse of the Victorian shirtwaist type. Its lace, tucks and buttons made one think of romantic settings. As Lindy kept saying, "First impressions are everything."

At her desk she pulled out a pile of paperwork, but found herself sitting and staring at her beautiful shop instead. Pale blue paint complemented subtly striped wallpaper. Brass-based Stiffel lamps gave light to the cloudy morning. New navy-blue sofas stood on the oriental rug, replacing the ratty old couch. Creig had claimed the ugly thing for his room, much to Mary's horror.

Everything was perfect, and Shelby felt satisfaction in knowing she had been right about the location. In the week she had been open at least a dozen people had stopped by to make inquiries. Noon, late afternoons and Saturdays seemed to be her best times. People from the office buildings and industrial complexes nearby spent a lot of time—and money—in Spanish Court. Its parklike setting, with its benches, fountains and outside eating areas, encouraged shoppers to linger.

Women customers, especially, were attracted to Featherstone Brides. Shelby already had her third clients. Two attorneys had come in for a consultation. Because their wedding was several months away, Shelby would have plenty of time to make arrangements.

It was vitally important that each wedding be as perfect as possible—for the bride and groom, for the fledgling reputation of Featherstone Brides but especially for Shelby's need to prove herself.

Lindy came out of the back room where she had been arranging gowns for the Barnes-Davis wedding. "I'll be so glad when that room is finished and I don't have to haul things back and forth," she sighed. "You can call Karla and tell her that she and her brides-maids can come try these on. How is everything else coming for her?''

''Fine. Although unfortunately, the entire stephan-otis crop has inexplicably decided to die. Mr. Budd assures me he can substitute something equally suit-able and, as he puts it, inoffensive.''

Lindy walked across the room and plopped onto the sofa with no apparent regard for its price tag. ''Inof-fensive, hmm? Are you sure its safe doing business with a florist named Budd?''

Shelby giggled. ''Seeing that his shop was named This Budd's For You, gave me second thoughts, but he is good at his job.''

''He's probably going to get himself sued by that beer company. Hey, how are Lynn's plans coming?''

''Slowly,'' Shelby answered, wrinkling her short nose. ''I can't seem to pin her down to a date. She keeps saying she'll know soon.''

''Wait till you see the design for Lynn's gown,'' Lindy said, rolling her eyes.

''Beautiful?''

''Mother's best,'' Lindy smiled proudly. ''I added a few suggestions, but Lynn had a very clear idea of what she wanted. Watered silk, lace, seed pearls...''

Shelby rearranged a stack of caterers' brochures. ''She has definite ideas on every other part of the wedding, too, right down to the flavor of the cake filling.''

''It doesn't seem that A.J. has a lot to say in these plans,'' Lindy observed, her keen eyes on her young-est sister.

Shelby grimaced. *That's what you think!* She held the stack of brochures upright and let them thump against the desk, aligning the top edges. "He's probably very busy."

Stretching like a feline, Lindy stood and picked up her purse. "Or maybe he isn't interested."

"Don't be silly, Lindy. It's his wedding, too," Shelby said briskly, although she knew his big interest was in putting Shelby out of a job.

"I've got to go. Nathan is probably terrorizing his baby-sitter. I'd better rescue her."

Shelby waved her sister off and went to straighten the mauve throw pillows Lindy had disarranged, then began organizing the bridal magazines on the coffee table, still thinking about A.J.

After their dinner on the beach, she had insisted he bring her back to her car. The ride was made in stony silence, with Shelby fuming over his attempt to buy her off. He had suggested she reconsider his offer, and she had slammed from the car in a huff. What really bothered her was knowing that, despite his animosity toward her, his engagement and her friendship with Lynn—in spite of it all—she couldn't deny the chemistry that flowed between them whenever they were together. She was attracted to him, and her own traitorous feelings sickened her.

Shelby finished lining the magazines up in a perfect fan. She plunked down on the sofa, disarranging the cushions she had just straightened. Leaning forward, she plopped her chin onto her palm. Was A.J.'s reluctance to have her involved in the wedding due to dislike? Or was it something else? And what about Lynn? Shelby shook her head. Lynn's whole attitude was so odd...eagerly making plans but not setting a date. Naturally Lynn had changed since her father's death, but she wasn't exhibiting grief now. Instead, she seemed to be in the grip of some kind of inner determination and excitement. Shelby never would have thought love would affect her formerly quiet and patient friend like that.

Shelby shook her head again and stood up. Her urge to nibble was getting the better of her, so she decided to close up for five minutes and dash down to the muffin shop in the mall. She was beginning to think the mall's convenient plaza style of architecture was a mistake. With everything so close she was having a hard time working off the extra calories she was consuming at the many eating establishments.

Minutes later, she was strolling back toward her shop with two plump blueberry muffins in a paper bag. A man was standing before Featherstone Brides, gazing in at the bridal gown displayed in the window. Lindy had used her own gown, carefully ironing out each crease and arranging it so that it looked ready to step into. Thinking the man must be a potential client, Shelby greeted him with her most winning smile. "Good morning, may I help you?"

He turned quickly and surveyed her, his dark brown eyes skipping over her form briefly before focusing on her face.

Startled by his lightning movement, Shelby backed up against the door. Something about his intensity alarmed her. Reaching back she put her hand on the doorknob. Too late she remembered the key was in her pocket. Her smile wavered uncertainly.

"You work here?" he asked, his eyes never leaving her face. He had an accent she couldn't quite place.

"Yes, I'm the owner...."

"Shelby Featherstone?"

"Why, yes. Have we met?"

He gazed at her for a moment from beneath thick, brooding brows before answering. "We have a mutual friend—Lynn Altman. I am Carlo Rosetti."

Shelby's eyes widened and she swallowed a gasp. Guiltily, her gaze darted around the mall as if she thought Lynn or A.J. might materialize from behind a potted palm.

A corner of his mouth quirked. "I see you have heard of me."

"Yes, uh, yes," she stammered.

"May I speak with you?" he asked.

The request was ultra-polite, but there was no denying the steely resolve behind it. He reminded her vaguely of A.J., although physically the two men were nothing alike. Carlo Rosetti was shorter, with wider shoulders. He had a shock of black hair and a high Roman nose. His eyes were a very dark brown and at the moment they were flickering impatiently. That *really* reminded her of A.J. Lynn sure knew how to pick them, Shelby thought on an inward sigh.

"Yes, please come in," she finally managed, turning to unlock the door. She waved him inside and indicated the sofas. "Sit down."

Instead, he looked down at the paper bag she carried. A delicious scent was emanating from it. He looked back at her curiously.

"Blueberry muffins," she blurted.

"Ah," he said, smiling. "Such an American food. I don't suppose you have...enough for two?" he asked with a hopeful smile.

He had a wonderful smile. It spread his lips wide, giving him an open, approachable look.

"As a matter of fact, I do," Shelby said, returning his smile. "Sit down. I've got fresh coffee made, too."

She scurried into the back room and poured two mugs of coffee while her mind ran through a dozen different reasons for his unexpected arrival. How had he heard about her? And what did he want?

When she reentered the main room, he was sitting on the sofa, leafing through a bridal magazine. Shelby couldn't imagine a more incongruous sight, considering what Lynn had told her about his aversion to marriage and commitment.

He dropped the magazine and stood to take the mug from her, then waited while she was seated. Shelby was impressed with his manners.

"You are wondering why I came," he stated when they were seated, biting into the muffin with evident enjoyment.

"Yes. How did you know about me?"

From the pocket of his Italian cut sports jacket, he took a newspaper clipping. She unfolded it to see Lynn and A.J.'s radiant faces smiling up at her. Randy Anderson's column describing the engagement party accompanied the photograph. The end of the article mentioned that all arrangements would be made by Shelby Featherstone. Shelby was pleased at the publicity but puzzled at how he had tracked her down.

"This article or an announcement just like it was in the Santa Barbara, Ventura and Los Angeles papers. When I saw the name of your shop, I knew you must be the one to talk to. Lynn has told me about you. You are her friend." Sight of the clipping seemed to cost him his appetite. He laid the muffin on a napkin and pushed it away.

"Since childhood," Shelby said, cautiously. "But what exactly do you want to know?"

He took the article and stared at it for a moment, his expression severe. He poked a finger into A.J.'s face. "I want to know about him. This man, Court. Do you know him?"

"Well, yes, I do, but I really don't think I should be discussing him with you. Have you talked to Lynn?"

"I want to hear from someone else," Carlo answered, his voice low and fierce, his eyes flashing. "Her view would be colored by—love." He practically spat the word. "What is he like?"

Shelby hesitated. He was going to insist if she didn't tell him.

"He was a friend of Lynn's father," she began. Carlo sat listening, his very stillness evidence of his concentration. "He's in real estate investing and development." She gestured toward the window. "He owns this mall and many other properties."

Carlo nodded, obviously filing away every shred of information. "But what is he like?"

Shelby racked her brain, trying to figure out exactly what he wanted her to say. "He's tall with dark hair and green eyes...."

"No, no, no!" Carlo shot to his feet and began pacing the room. "I want to know what kind of man he is."

Shelby watched him prowl restlessly between her desk and the window. "You mean you want to know if he's good enough for Lynn?"

He stopped and gave her a straightforward look that became a bit sheepish. With a half-apologetic nod he agreed.

Shelby gazed at him in dismay. She had the feeling he wouldn't go until she told him what he wanted to know. She took a deep breath.

"A.J. Court comes from a very poor background, but he has made himself successful. He's persistent." Ruefully, she thought of his insistence that she quit the wedding. Persistence didn't say half of it. "He's single-minded but fair, I think." She thought of Erica. "He will do almost anything for someone he loves." She tilted her head, considering that thought. "Helpful and sympathetic, I guess you might say." No, it went beyond that. "Compassionate."

"A wimp," Carlo snorted, tossing his head like an angry bull.

"Not at all!" Shelby declared, incensed.

"It sounds as if he has made another conquest besides Lynn." Carlo's eyes were shrewd.

Color ran up under Shelby's skin. She hadn't meant to be so transparent. "I simply think he's a good man, with a sense of responsibility."

Furiously, Carlo paced toward her. "And Lynn has told you I have none?"

"No! She never said anything like that!"

"Is that why she dumped me?"

Shelby blinked in confusion. "She dumped *you*?"

His powerful shoulders heaved upward. "She might as well have. She refused to see me again unless I was considering a future for us."

And he didn't like ultimatums, Shelby finished for him silently. Her heart went out to him although she felt terribly guilty about discussing Lynn and A.J. with him. "Do you really think you should tell me—" she began, but his Latin temper was on fire.

"She doesn't seem to understand I may not *have* a future." He threw his hands out in front of him for her inspection. "This is all I have. Racing. No big investments. All my winnings go back to my pit crew, my car, entrance fees.... I don't even have a real home. I have nothing to offer someone like her.''

Just yourself, Shelby thought, realizing how attractive his excitable, passionate nature would be to someone like Lynn, who had been so protected all her life. She squirmed uncomfortably, realizing the discussion was pointless. ''I think this is probably a moot question,'' she said.

He frowned, his thick black brows drawing together as he concentrated on her. ''Moot? I don't know that word.''

Her hands lifted helplessly as she tried to decide how to describe it to him. ''It means hypothetical. Something that's not likely to happen.''

Carlo's suddenly fierce look had Shelby shrinking back against the sofa.

''Not likely to happen? Ha! We'll see about that!'' He swept out the door, leaving Shelby gasping as if she had just been picked up and dropped by a tornado.

She slumped against the sofa cushions and theatrically put the back of her wrist to her forehead. The man was like a seething volcano. No wonder his relationship with Lynn had been rocky. Lynn!

Shelby leaped for the telephone, wanting to warn Lynn that Carlo was in town and would probably try to contact her. She punched out the number, but there was no answer at the Altmans' home. She considered calling A.J., but she didn't know what to say. Look out, your fiancée's old boyfriend is gunning for you hardly seemed appropriate. Mind your own business, Shelby, she told herself, putting down the phone. Lynn was an adult. She could handle this herself. So could A.J.

Shelby spent a busy afternoon answering customers' questions, making phone calls and coordi-
nating the fittings for Karla's bridesmaids. By the time
Mary arrived to do the fittings, Shelby was ready to
drop. In spite of her good intentions to mind her own
business, Shelby thought about Lynn and A.J. and of
the two disagreements she had heard them have.
Considering it, she thought the last one had concerned Lynn placing the announcement in the Los
Angeles papers. A.J. probably feared that Carlo
would see it—and he had.

Quietly, she went about helping her mother with the
fittings and writing down exact measurements for the
alterations. There weren't that many. Being the
craftswoman she was, Mary had been able to fit the
dresses almost perfectly even though most of the
bridesmaids had been to only one previous fitting.

That night, after she and her mother had finished
the dishes, Mary went to her sewing machine and
Shelby wandered into her room. She sat in the small
rocker by the window, another legacy from Great
Aunt Laura, and stared out at the peach tree that was
beginning to lose its leaves.

Carlo's visit had left her in a haze of confusion. He
seemed so determined and hot-tempered, she couldn't
predict what he might do. Maybe nothing, but he
would surely upset Lynn, she thought, recalling a
phone call she had received from her friend the previous spring. Lynn had been in San Diego with her
mother. Carlo had visited her there. They had fought,
and Lynn had called Shelby to talk about it.

It could happen again. Although Lynn was going to
marry A.J., Carlo could still have the power to upset

her. Feelings as strong as the ones Lynn had held for Carlo didn't die overnight.

Her decision made, Shelby stood up suddenly. She would go to see Lynn. They could talk over a cup of hot chocolate, just like old times.

She quietly slipped out the door to avoid Creig's questions about her destination and climbed into her car, heading straight to the Altmans'.

Arriving at the big house Lynn was now occupying with only the housekeeper, Shelby eagerly rang the doorbell. When Mrs. Moran answered and said Lynn wasn't home, Shelby grimaced and slumped against the door frame.

"I should have called first," she sighed.

Mrs. Moran clucked sympathetically. "But you ran out of the house without thinking."

"You know me too well."

Mrs. Moran's smile faded into a pinched look. "Lynn has a fiancé now, so she's gone a lot."

"Is she at A.J.'s now?"

"You mean Mr. Court? I think so. She got a phone call and left without saying anything to me."

Shelby heard the hurt behind the words but didn't know what to make of it. She pushed away from the door frame. "I can talk to her later." She started to turn away.

"You could probably go on over to Mr. Court's," Mrs. Moran volunteered. "He's been teaching her how to cook."

Shelby stopped halfway down the front stairs and looked back over her shoulder, her eyes wide in amazement. "He's teaching her to *cook*?"

The pinched look tightened. "That's right."

"Why aren't *you* teaching her?"

The housekeeper looked appalled. "And have someone messing up my kitchen?"

Shelby remembered how protective Mrs. Moran was. Mrs. Altman had never cooked, so helping out hadn't been an issue with her.

"I'm still cleaning up the mess those caterers made at that—engagement party."

The unusual bitterness of her tone had Shelby swinging around and hurrying back up the stairs. She laid her hand on Mrs. Moran's arm. "What's wrong?" she asked. "Are you upset about Lynn's engagement."

Mrs. Moran pursed her lips. "Not the engagement. Mr. Court is a fine man. It's the way Lynn is going about it. She could at least let her own mother in on the wedding plans."

"But Mrs. Altman has been so upset," Shelby defended. "She doesn't want to come back here...."

Mrs. Moran gave her a pitying look. "Do you really think Mrs. Altman wouldn't hurry back here and put her own feelings aside to be with Lynn at a time like this? Especially since Lynn is marrying someone she and Mr. Altman liked so much?" She wagged her finger at Shelby. "Mark my words—" Then she drew herself up. "But it's not for me to discuss my employer's business. Nobody asked my opinion." She hurried into the house and closed the door, leaving Shelby with her mind spinning.

Her hand gripping the rail, Shelby descended the steps and climbed into her Rabbit. Fingering her keys, she stared through the windshield. Mrs. Moran was right. It *was* odd that Lynn's mother wasn't involved. Many things about Lynn's behavior seemed odd. Maybe Lynn wasn't really serious about marriage? No, that wasn't possible. Lynn had always wanted a marriage exactly like the happy one her parents had.

Shelby chewed her bottom lip. But what if all these plans fell through? she thought in despair. Not only would she take a financial loss, but her reputation might suffer. Shelby winced at the thought of her mother putting in weeks of work on Lynn's elaborate gown, only to have it go unused.

Now she *really* needed to talk to Lynn, but she hesitated, remembering her last encounter with A.J. Each time she saw him, things seemed to go from bad to worse. And she was still burning from his attempt to force her out of the wedding plans. Nevertheless, she had to talk to Lynn. She shoved the key into the ignition and started the motor.

A.J.'s address was on a card at the shop. All of her clients—the six of them—were neatly typed onto Rolodex cards.

But his was the only address she had memorized. It was a couple of miles down one of the winding roads near the Altmans'.

It was beginning to get dark by the time she located the house set back in a stand of pine trees. She was surprised to see that the structure wasn't the model of perfection she would have expected. Lumber and bags of cement were stacked neatly in the front yard. Either A.J. was having renovations done or the place was still under construction. Lynn's small white Triumph sports car was nowhere to be seen, but Shelby thought it might be garaged.

Shelby stepped gingerly around the building materials. He was only adding to the house, she decided. If the cedar siding was any indication, the place had been standing for a number of years. It had weathered to an attractive gray color that made the place look rustic.

Shelby recalled the elegant furnishings and the collection of crystal in A.J.'s office. His home was worlds different. She wondered which one reflected the real Alexander Court.

There was no answer to her knock on the front door, so Shelby stepped back and studied the windows. All were dark except for the one to her right. It appeared to have a faint glow as if a light were on in the back of the house, probably in the kitchen.

She picked her way around the house and was startled to see a gardener pushing a wheelbarrow of dirt up an incline covered with a succulent ground cover of ice plant. The man was bent double over the handles of the barrow. In the gathering dusk it took Shelby several seconds to realize she was looking at A. J. Court.

She watched as he strained behind the load, trying to keep the wheelbarrow steady on its one front wheel. Amused, she looked around at the lushly planted yard. Apparently it was easier to take the boy off the farm than to take the farm out of the boy.

A.J. had almost reached the top of the incline and was preparing to set the wheelbarrow down.

"You could hire someone to do that, you know," she called.

A.J. started and whipped around. He hadn't let go of the wheelbarrow as she had thought but still retained his hold on the handles. Horrified, she watched as his feet slipped on the water-filled succulents. He and the wheelbarrow started back down the hill much faster than they'd gone up.

"Oh—!" A.J. broke off on a curse as he and the wheelbarrow careened down. He fought to keep his footing and hold the load of dirt upright, but dirt sifted over the sides with each correction A.J. made to the careening flight.

Shelby dropped her purse and started forward to try to prevent the disaster she had caused.

When she reached him, she made a grab for the handles, but he yelled, "Stay back!"

Obediently, she jumped aside and watched as A.J.'s heel hit a rock and his feet began to slide out from under him. He stubbornly held on, obviously hoping he could keep the load upright, but his body was stretched out like a rubber band about to snap. Too late he freed his hands but couldn't help himself as he fell face forward into the ice plant. He managed to roll over a couple of times to avoid the wheel.

Before he could get up, the wheelbarrow slid back a few more feet, wobbled, tilted and with a soft whoosh, deposited its load of soil on top of A.J.'s fallen figure. The wheelbarrow itself followed with a thump.

CHAPTER SEVEN

SHELBY DASHED to where A.J. was buried beneath the load of dirt. She grabbed the wheelbarrow and wrestled it away.

"A.J.! Are you all right?" she yelled, frantically scrabbling at the dirt that covered his head.

What if he had suffocated? The dirt was so fine it could have packed into his nose and mouth. Oh, why hadn't she taken first aid or CPR at the Red Cross?

With a stifled moan the pile of dirt began to tremble and roll like an earthquake. Shelby flung away handfuls of soil and helped A.J. turn onto his back.

In the deepening night she could barely distinguish his dirt-caked features.

"Hi," she said inanely. "Are you okay?"

A.J. gave her a look she was glad she couldn't see too clearly, and struggled to sit up. When he spoke, his voice was controlled, but Shelby knew he was furious. He wiped the dirt off his face and plucked a purple ice plant bloom from behind his ear. "Except for having twenty pounds of dirt down the back of my neck, I'm fine. Don't tell me—" he went on carefully. "You've found a more suitable property somewhere else—Timbuktu, I hope—and you came to turn in your key." He ended on a hopeful note.

"Uh, no."

"You were just passing by...."

She bit her lip and swallowed a hysterical giggle. "I wouldn't dare resort to clichés at a time like this."

"Wise of you."

"A.J., can you stand up?"

"Not until you get off my right foot."

"Oh, excuse me." Shelby hopped up and stood back. As she dusted some of the streaks off her pink skirt, she watched him heave himself to his feet. He shook his head and body like a dog after its bath.

Dirt flew everywhere, but there was still a considerable amount of it on him. "I'm going to go into the house now." His careful tone was splintered with ice. "I'm going to take a shower. I'm going to eat dinner and then you can tell me what you came for."

Eyes wide, Shelby started backing away, slipping and sliding on the plants the two of them had crushed. "That's all right," she stammered. "Forget it. I was just looking for Lynn. I'll speak to her some other time. I'll call her at home—or your office, make an appointment with Miss, uh, well whatever her name is...."

"Why start something new?" he grumbled, coming after her. His broad hand wrapped around her arm. "Oh, no you don't. You're coming inside."

"Don't you want to clean up this mess?" she asked, stalling.

He didn't even glance down. "You're the one who should clean it up," he countered, pulling her toward the back door. "I was trying to finish that section before dark, but..."

Outside the kitchen, he pulled off his white T-shirt and used it to dust himself off. He leaned over and ruffled his hands through his hair. Again, dirt flew and Shelby stepped back.

A.J. caught the movement out of the corner of his eye and grabbed for her arm again. "If you try to leave, I'll come to your house and get you," he growled. "Remember, I know where you live. Come on." He hustled her inside.

In the kitchen he let go of her and pointed to a chair pulled up to a round oak table. "Sit down and don't move until I get out of the shower." He shot her a sardonic look. "Unless you want to watch."

Shelby lifted her chin, ignoring his ungentlemanly reminder of her visit to his office. To show him she had every intention of staying where he had told her to sit, she arranged herself primly on the chair he had indicated.

He watched her maneuvering, snorted and stomped from the room.

As soon as he was out of sight, Shelby looked around eagerly. In all her life she had never seen a room she had fallen in love with so instantly and completely.

A.J.'s kitchen was a virtual greenhouse! The ceiling was one huge series of skylights, but instead of the standard square or rectangular shape, these formed a fan. The hub of the fan was over the kitchen sink and the spokes went out over the room. Plant holders hung from the ceiling, sat on shelves, even trailed from the top of the refrigerator. She knew that during the day light must pour in on the dozens of plants in the room.

She had been right about one thing. He was a farmer at heart. And wrong about another—his collection of crystal did extend to his home. Only here it was bells lined up on shelves that ran at eye level around the room. He owned all sizes of bells, plain ones, fancy ones, some smaller than the tip of her finger, some larger than dinner bells.

She disobeyed A.J.'s order by standing and walking over to inspect the collection, then made a circuit of the rest of the room, which was about twenty feet across. Her mother would love having a kitchen this big. There were what seemed like acres of counter space and even a work island. She wondered if A.J. used all the appliances lined up on the counter or if he had bought them for Lynn's cooking lessons.

Anxious to explore the rest of the house she started toward the dining room.

"I knew you couldn't stay put," a voice growled behind her.

A.J. stood in the doorway. His hair was still damp and he was barefoot in clean jeans and a white shirt. He was rolling up the sleeves with quick efficient turns of his wrist.

She decided to graciously ignore his comment. "This is a beautiful room. Did you design it?"

A.J. couldn't disguise the look of quiet pride that crossed his face as he turned and walked toward the refrigerator. "With an architect."

"Tell me, where are you going to live when the plants take over?"

He swung the refrigerator door open, keeping his back to her. "You don't like it?"

"Actually, I love it," she admitted, winning a look of pleasure from him. When he turned back to his task, she glanced down at her hands and took a deep breath. "A.J., I'm sorry that I surprised you a while ago. I just didn't think...."

He glanced over his shoulder again. "That seems to be a chronic condition with you."

She winced, although she didn't blame him for being exasperated with her. Once again she had jumped headfirst into something she should have avoided. "Well," she said heartily. "You know that my dad always tells me to go with my feelings."

"Lead with your heart, hmm?" he asked, taking an ovenproof glass dish from the freezer and placing it in the microwave. He set the dial and turned back to her. "Does this philosophy get you into trouble with other people, or am I the only lucky one?"

Shelby rubbed her nose with the back of her hand. "Lately you're the only one," she admitted.

"Okay, what riot of emotions, what upheaval of distress brought you here tonight? On second thought, don't tell me yet. This sounds like another example of carpe diem. I think I'd better eat first. I may need my strength. Would you like some?"

It took Shelby a few moments to realize he wasn't talking about his strength but the food that she could now smell, sending its wonderful scent into the room. "No, thanks. I've eaten."

He smiled enticingly. "I made it myself—chicken casserole."

"I've heard you can cook, that you're even teaching Lynn."

"You sound surprised," A.J. said sardonically. "Who says chauvinism is dead?"

"I'm not being chauvinistic. I'm just surprised that you're teaching Lynn."

"Why? I can cook. She can't. She wants to learn. Thinks the way to a man's heart is through his stomach."

"But not yours?" Shelby asked cautiously, aware that she was dragging out the conversation because she didn't know if she should tell him about Carlo's visit.

A.J. shrugged at her last remark, and she decided to keep quiet about her visitor until she had talked to Lynn.

The microwave timer buzzed and A.J. picked up a couple of pot holders to carry his steaming dinner to the table. He returned to the refrigerator for a beer.

Shelby smiled at that. He didn't seem like a beer drinker. She thought wine or champagne would be more his style. "You don't have to cook, you could eat at Erica's."

"Not for a while," he answered easily, tucking into his dinner. "I want to put off having to explain my two fiancées as long as possible."

She smiled at that and relaxed into her chair. She enjoyed remembering his friends and their affection for him. He inspired their loyalty, and they had his. There seemed to be a basic integrity about him that she found as appealing as his slow, sexy smile and quick mind.

Shelby also enjoyed watching him eat. His motions were sparing and efficient. He didn't spend a lot of time seasoning his food and arranging it just right. He simply ate.

She didn't realize how long she had been sitting and staring at him until A.J. put down his fork and looked at her—just looked—for long moments as she had been doing. His gaze touched on each of her features, the perfect oval of her face, eyes that were wide with curiosity, lips that started to tremble even as he watched. His own harshly handsome features softened, his left-sided dimple appearing as he leaned forward. The handle of his fork was still pointed at her. He drew it downward as if marking a line down the center of her body. Shelby shivered as a wave of heat washed down the valley between her breasts.

A.J.'s voice was low and thrumming with innuendos that she couldn't mistake. "If there's anything you want to know about me, Shelby, all you have to do is ask."

His words and the sexy tone of his voice filled her mind with such erotic images that she blushed and gasped, "Why do you *do* that?"

He sat back, looking faintly curious. "Do what?"

He was playing games with her. But why? His attitude didn't add up with the way she knew him to be. By playing games and flirting with her he could hurt Lynn. Shelby couldn't believe he would want to do that to Lynn—but he didn't seem to mind hurting her, instead.

Her puzzlement at his actions gave way to plain fury. If he couldn't get her to resign from the wedding arrangements with bribery, he would try frightening her away with his blatant sexuality. Hard on the heels of that angry thought was the realization that her own attraction to him must be very obvious or he wouldn't think of trying such a method.

Full of loathing for herself—and him—she stood up shakily, her pleasant gamine features a mask of hurt and shock. "I'll be going. I thought Lynn was here. I wanted to talk to her."

His gaze never left hers as he stood up, hope lighting his face. "Then you are going to tell Lynn to find someone else to arrange the wedding?"

"Why are you so insistent? No matter what you may believe, I'll do a good job."

He tossed his fork down onto his plate with a clatter. His hand lifted to run around the back of his neck. His face was set, but in it she saw a flicker of concern. "I've told you before, Shelby. It's just not a good idea." A weary sigh expelled from between his tight lips. "Damn it! I don't want you to get hurt."

"Do you know where Lynn is?"

The shop door shuddered on its hinges as A.J. swept in. He shut the door with a thud that rattled the glass, and rushed over to Shelby's desk.

She jumped, smearing ink across the wedding plan sheet she was working up for a new client. "Where Lynn is?"

She had left A.J.'s house the night before, puzzled and distraught over his statement that he didn't want her to be hurt. What could hurt her and why did he care? His only concern had seemed to be that she pull out of the wedding arrangements. Last night he had seemed so genuine. Unless that was another ploy like their dinner on the beach.

"Yes. Did you find her last night? She didn't come home, and Mrs. Moran is worried."

Immediately the image of Carlo flashed into her mind. For an instant she wondered if he had hurt Lynn, but she dismissed that idea. He seemed hot-headed but not crazy. Lynn might be hiding from him, though. Why wouldn't she have turned to A.J. for help, then?

"No," Shelby said, carefully avoiding his eyes as she dabbed at the ink streaking across her planning sheet. "I don't know where she is. I didn't find her last night." She hesitated then sighed. "But...someone else might have.'' Slowly, knowing she should have done so before, she told him about Carlo's visit.

As she talked, A.J.'s expression became more and more grim as if something was twisting inside him. His mouth angled down and his brows pulled together in irritation. "This happened yesterday?'' he demanded to know, sweeping back the sides of his jacket and thrusting out his chin.

"Yes.'' Shelby twisted her fingers through the strand of pearls at her throat.

"And you were looking for Lynn to tell her about him?'' A.J.'s finger stabbed the air an inch from her nose.

Shelby's eyes almost crossed as she gazed at the blunt-tipped finger ready to put a dent in the end of her nose. "Yes,'' she said, lifting her gaze to his.

He flipped his hand impatiently and began pacing. She watched his feet circuit the room in the same path Carlo's had followed the day before.

"Why the hell didn't you tell me last night?''

"Because I knew you would react just as you're doing now!'' she snapped. "You continually think the worst of me,'' Shelby said in her own defense, coming out from behind the desk and beginning to pace. "I was afraid you would think I was meddling since I'm . . . well . . . impulsive sometimes.'' She ignored his snort of agreement. "I didn't mean to get involved, but I got dragged into this situation.''

"That's the truth,'' A.J. muttered, casting her a dark look as he crossed in front of her.

"I was trying to warn Lynn!'' she said, striding from the desk to the window while he prowled from the front door to the back room doorway. Their paths crossed again near the sofa.

"I don't think the worst of you," he growled. "I just don't want you mixed up in this. Hell, I wish Lynn hadn't—"

"Well, I am mixed up in this—this, whatever it is. Hadn't what?" Shelby asked, turning on the heel of her gray suede pump.

"Never mind." He stopped directly in front of the door. If someone had opened the shop door at that moment, he would have been knocked flat on his face. Shelby took a perverse pleasure in the thought.

"I wish you would finish your sentences. You make these puzzling statements and never finish what you were going to say."

"You don't want to know—and besides, you keep cutting me off."

"If I didn't want to know, I wouldn't ask!" When he didn't reply, Shelby gritted her teeth in frustration. "Do you think Carlo found her?"

A.J. sighed and rolled his eyes heavenward. "I should be so lucky."

Shelby clamped her hands on her hips. "You think seeing him will get him out of her system once and for all?"

"Let's just say it might settle things," he said enigmatically. "Come on, we've got to find her."

"We?" Shelby asked cautiously.

Turning, he began to pace again. "Yes, we'll have to brainstorm to come up with some idea of where she is. I'm responsible for her."

"A.J., she's a grown woman," Shelby said, slipping her hands into the pockets of the gray suede jacket that matched her skirt. "She's responsible for herself."

Her steady gaze watched his restless pacing around the room. She was worried, too, about Lynn's state of mind.

"Does she have a favorite place she likes to go when she needs to think?" he asked.

"Maybe the Altmans' summer cabin?" Shelby suggested, chewing her lip thoughtfully.

He stopped his restless measuring of the room. "You mean the condo on Maui?"

"No, it's an old rustic cabin where they used to go a lot when Lynn was little. She loves it there, but I don't think the family has been there together in ages. Certainly not in the past year."

"Never heard of it." He drew a pen and small pad from his jacket pocket. "Is it near here? Give me directions."

Shelby frowned, her blue eyes thoughtful. It was strange that he didn't know about the cabin. He had been helping Mrs. Altman with financial matters since her husband's death. Perhaps mention of the cabin had simply never come up. "It's in the Angeles National Forest above San Bernardino. Very remote. Near Big Bear actually, about four hours from here."

A sigh of exasperation gusted through A.J.'s teeth. "Have you been there?"

"Years ago. We went skiing."

"What makes you think she would be there now?"

Shelby shrugged. "She's always loved it. The mountains are her favorite place to be. She once told me she would like to live there year-round."

"Do you know the phone number?" he asked, moving toward the telephone.

"No phone. I told you, it's remote—and rustic. Anyway, what exactly do you plan to say to her when you get there?"

"You're the impetuous one. I'll just take a leaf from your book and say whatever seems right for the moment." A sudden smile, devilishly intent, broke over his face. "Carpe diem, remember?"

She was getting mortally sick of him throwing that phrase at her but before she could think of an appropriately scathing response, his smile disappeared and he nodded decisively. "All right, you'll have to guide me to the cabin." He swept around her desk, heading for the telephone. "I'll call my office and tell them I'll be gone the rest of the day. Can you get someone to come in and watch the shop while you're gone, or do you just want to close up for the day? I realize it's an inconvenience since it's only 2:00 p.m., but it can't be helped."

"Guide you?" Shelby sputtered. "Close up shop?"

"Of course," he said, his green eyes regarding her as if he had made a perfectly reasonable request. "I may not be able to find the place on my own and by the time I get there, it will be almost dark."

"But I can't go, I've got a client coming...."

"Change it," he commanded, punching out his office number on her phone.

Shelby listened in growing frustration as he spoke to Miss Simmons. She might as well go, she decided. He wasn't going to let her stay behind. Besides, she was worried about Lynn, too, and Mrs. Moran must be beside herself. How on earth had she gotten into the middle of this? she wondered as she looked up the number of the young woman doctor with whom she had a three o'clock appointment. "If I lose business over this, it'll be your fault, A. J. Court," she grumbled.

"I'm willing to make it worth your while," he said, handing the phone over to her with a smirk.

She almost threw it at him.

Arrangements were quickly made for Lindy to reopen the shop, and Shelby was able to reschedule her appointment with the prospective client. A.J. tapped his foot impatiently as she locked up then whisked her out to the Jaguar. They made it to San Bernardino in record time, even through the crush of traffic. During the drive Shelby kept looking furtively over her shoulder, expecting them to be stopped by a highway patrolman at any moment. It would serve him right, she thought. But luck was on the side of the reckless, and A.J. had no problems as he raced down the freeways.

By the time they reached the mountains, clouds were lowering, and Shelby glanced worriedly at the sky. She hoped it didn't rain. It would make their drive home that much more difficult later that night.

A.J. slowed as she gave directions to the cabin perched on a cliff rim several miles from the town of Big Bear. An encroaching fog made it difficult for them to find their way. However, mountain vacations had been few and far between in a family where every penny had to do double duty so Shelby vividly remembered every moment of her time at the Altmans' cabin, including the way along the winding roads.

Both of them slumped in disappointment when they finished jolting over the rutted drive and stopped before a cabin that had the name Altman painted on a small plaque beside the door. Lynn's car wasn't parked out front, and there were no lights on against the gathering dusk and steadily worsening fog.

"Now what?" Shelby asked.

A.J. was already sliding out from under the wheel. "Now we find a way to get inside to see if she's been here."

"You mean breaking and entering?" Shelby gasped. "That's against the law."

"I'll have a locksmith come out first thing in the morning to fix whatever we damage."

"Oh, great," Shelby fumed, getting out of the car and following him to the front door. "It's not enough that you make me leave my shop and come up here on a wild-goose chase, but now you're making me an accessory to a crime!"

"I can cook, remember. I'll send you a cake with a file in it if you're thrown into jail," A.J. told her unsympathetically as he ran his hands over the knob and the dead-bolt lock. "Think of this as just deserts for dumping that load of dirt on me."

Shelby sent him a mutinous look and watched as he searched all around the edges of the doorway. He grunted in satisfaction when he discovered the key under a loose board of the porch. "I'll have to talk to Sharon Altman about this. It's very careless."

"No kidding," Shelby said earnestly. "She should be more careful. There's no telling what kind of riff-raff might just walk in."

A.J. scowled at her, turned the key in the lock and pushed the door open.

Shelby's gaze raked eagerly around the room, but A.J. stood for a moment on the porch, frowning back at the fog.

Shelby took off her jacket and laid it with her purse on a table by the door. Delighted, she saw that the cabin was just as she remembered it.

As always, Mrs. Altman's superb taste showed even in a home seldom used. The furniture, a sofa facing the huge fireplace and several easy chairs, was heavy but simple. The dark-stained floor was complemented by red and yellow braided rugs and roughly plastered white walls. The cabin had only one bedroom and a tiny bathroom. The place felt cozy and unpretentious, very different from the Altmans' Santa Barbara home.

"Where's the light switch?" A.J. asked, feeling along the wall.

"Guess again," Shelby answered, making her way cautiously through the gathering gloom toward a small table by the window.

"What do you mean?"

She picked up a kerosene lamp and a box of matches and held them up. "I told you it was rustic. Do you know how to light one of these?"

"Are you kidding?" he asked gruffly, whisking the items from her hands. "I hardly knew what electricity was until I was six."

Embarrassed, Shelby turned away. Glancing about for any signs of recent habitation, she ran her fingers over the mantel, then the hearth. The fireplace was swept clean and logs laid in place. Only the touch of a match was needed to send the logs into crackling flame. A fine layer of dust lay over the hearth area, showing no evidence of a recent fire. She decided the wood must have been there since the Altmans' last visit.

A small kerosene camp stove stood in a corner of the room, along with an icebox that required a huge chunk of ice to keep things cold. Both stood open and empty.

As A.J. lit the lamp and adjusted the wick, she could see that the pantry doors were tightly closed and that no empty cans were in the trash container.

"Well, I guess that answers our question," she sighed, turning to him. "Lynn hasn't been here. We'd better— What are you doing?" she asked, when she saw he was bending down before the fireplace.

"Lighting the fire, obviously."

"But we've got to go. It's getting dark!"

He sighed, his lips flattening in a rueful grimace. "I'm afraid we're not going anywhere for a while. Look at that fog." He nodded toward the window.

Automatically, her gaze followed his. Outside the world was covered with a thick, white blanket.

CHAPTER EIGHT

"BUT WE CAN'T STAY HERE." Her voice rose with a tinge of hysteria. "I thought you were so worried about Lynn."

"I am." He knelt at the hearth and struck a match to the wood. Within moments tongues of fire licked up to take possession of the seasoned wood. It began to sizzle and crackle cheerfully, warding off the chill of early fall.

A.J. stretched his hands toward the blaze. His head dropped forward and he let his shoulders slouch. Shelby was touched by the vulnerable set of his shoulders.

Nervousness began to sizzle and crackle not so cheerfully along her spine. "If we don't go right now the fog will just get worse. I've got to get back...."

"We can't drive in that, Shelby. We'll have to wait until it clears a little. We can't take a chance on unfamiliar roads...."

"You should have thought of that before you dragged me up here!"

"How was I supposed to know this would happen?" he snapped, then seeing her genuine distress, he softened. "The fog might let up any minute and we'll have a better chance of getting out of here safely."

"*I'm* getting out of here now," she said, grabbing up her jacket and purse and wheeling toward the door with some vague idea of making her way to the main highway.

"Shelby, wait!"

Frightened, she looked back to see A.J. bolt after her like a track star at the starting gun. His headlong charge spurred her to hurry. She swung the door open and started down the unlit steps damp from the dew-laden fog.

Shelby's low-heeled pumps slipped and she teetered for a moment on the edge of the top step. When her arms flew wide, as she tried to regain her balance, her jacket and purse went flying in one direction and her feet in the other. With several sickening bumps, she tumbled to the bottom of the steps.

A.J. was beside her in seconds. "Shelby, are you all right?" His voice sounded shaken.

"I think so."

"Once, just once, I wish you'd think before you act."

The gentle touch of his hands as he ran them over her checking for injuries belied his grumpy tone. She gasped and jerked away when he touched her left knee and when he got to her arm, his hand came away bloody.

"Ooooh," she moaned, closing her eyes.

"You can't tell me you're one of those women who faints at the sight of blood."

"Of course I am. That's *my* blood. But I'm used to it," she said with a sigh, struggling to sit up.

It was getting too dark to see clearly, but she could tell from his voice that he was grinning as he helped her to sit up, "Lots of scrapes as a kid, huh?"

"The companies that make adhesive bandages of-fered to make Mom a member of their board of directors because she bought so many of their products for me," she answered brightly to cover her embarrassment at her own stupidity. "Until I was twelve I thought I had been born with Merthiolate orange knees."

"Well, it looks like your knee got it again, but it must not be too bad if you can make jokes about it. Let's get you inside. That's a nasty scrape."

He looped her arm around his neck and slipped his arms beneath her.

Shelby clutched at him as he swept her into his arms, turned and headed back up the stairs.

He deposited her carefully onto the couch, took off his jacket and rolled up his shirtsleeves. "What do they do for water around here?"

"There's an electric pump outside."

A.J. lurched in surprise. "There's no electricity inside, but there's an electric pump outside? I guess Sanford and Sharon's idea of roughing it didn't extend to doing without running water and a bathroom."

"Yes, Mrs. Altman says roughing it has its limits." With her good arm, Shelby gestured toward the kitchen drawers. "The pump used to have a padlock on it. I think the key was kept somewhere in one of those drawers."

A.J. rustled in the drawers until he found the key, and went outside to turn on the pump. In a few minutes he had the water on and a basin filled with icy water. He found washcloths in the bathroom, soaked them and brought them to her. She lifted herself against the sofa back and rolled up her torn and bloodstained sleeve.

A.J. knelt beside her, placed a cold cloth on her knee, and started wiping off the worst of the blood on her arm.

"You're going to have to take that off," he told her, leaning back on his heels.

Her blue eyes huge, Shelby gazed up at him. "You mean my blouse?"

"Of course," he answered matter-of-factly. "It's ruined, and the dried blood is just going to stick to your sores."

Shelby clutched the neck of her blouse with her good hand.

A.J. sat back on his heels and gave her a smile that grew into a full-sized grin. "Why, Miss Featherstone, you don't think I have designs on your honor, do you?"

"Well, n-no, but—"

"Then take it off, or I will."

"You'll have to find me something else to wear."

"Like what? A bedsheet?"

"I don't know!" she snapped, feeling ridiculous. "Look in the bedroom. Maybe Mrs. Altman or Lynn left some clothes."

With an aggrieved sigh, A.J. got to his feet and went into the bedroom. Shelby heard a great deal of drawer opening, door slamming and muttering. Finally he came out with two pieces of cloth clutched in his hands. He held up the first one. "How about this?"

Shelby gasped. It was a black lace nightgown. The size was large enough to tell her it belonged to Mrs. Altman, a stout woman, and not to Lynn, but the style was straight out of Frederick's of Hollywood. She had to admit, though, that it was a marvel of engineering—if it actually stayed on the wearer's shoulders. It plunged front and back and would have reached far past Shelby's navel and spine. The elongated V was held together with thin black ribbons. The creation had the tiniest of spaghetti straps but enough frothy black lace around the hem to clothe a chorus line.

"I can't wear that!"

A.J. looked at it admiringly. "Can you imagine *Sharon* wearing it?" he asked in tones of awe.

Their eyes met and they burst into simultaneous whoops of laughter as they pictured the dignified woman in the sexy gown.

"In black spike heels," Shelby offered, embroidering their mental picture. When their laughter died down, she scolded, "We'd better not talk about her like that. She'll haunt us and besides, she's your future mother-in-law."

He sobered and tossed the gown back inside the bedroom. "Well, how about this thing, then?"

It was a Mickey Mouse T-shirt, probably a relic from Lynn's college days.

"It'll look perfect with my suede skirt," Shelby assured him.

He handed it over and turned his back without being asked. To her embarrassment Shelby discovered she couldn't maneuver her sore arm out of her torn sleeve. "A.J.?"

"My eyes are closed, Lady Godiva."

She cleared her throat. "I need help."

He swung around. Seeing her flushed face and averted eyes he made quick but careful work of getting her into the shirt. Shelby repressed a shiver as his fingers touched her arm. When they finally had the shirt arranged, A.J. rolled up the sleeve to expose her upper arm and picked up the basin of water.

Turning her toward the light A.J. clucked his tongue in distress.

"What is it?"

"I didn't see this before, but you picked up several large splinters from that porch step."

"Splinters? How big?"

"Does the size matter?"

"I just want to know, is it one you can barely see with the naked eye?"

"A little larger than that . . . and there are several of them."

She groaned. "You mean the kind where people say 'Hold still while I pull out this teeny-tiny sliver. Maybe we can sell it to someone who needs a mast for a clipper ship.' That kind of splinter?"

"My, how you exaggerate," he said admiringly, getting to his feet. "They're not that big—not quite. I'll have to see if I can find a pair of pliers, I mean tweezers, or a needle."

At the word "needle" Shelby sank with a moan into the sofa cushions, then gasped because she had involuntarily bent her sore knee.

He was back in a moment with the tweezers. Just as he was about to touch them to her skin, she reached up and grabbed his wrist. "I'd better warn you, A.J., I'm not good with pain."

"The girl who kept Johnson & Johnson in Band-Aid profits, afraid of pain? I don't believe it." His teasing tone softened, as did his look. "Don't worry," he said, reaching up to run his finger down her cheek. "I'll take care of you."

Shelby was so bemused by his tenderness that she barely noticed when he plucked out the slivers, but she emitted a soft squeal when the ice-cold cloth touched her ravaged skin.

"Sorry." A.J. winced. "There's a water heater for the bathroom, but it's not hot yet."

"That's all right," she mumbled, watching as he blotted at her skin. His hands were gentle, and she thought of how carefully he had held little Becky. Then unbidden, she thought of how he had kissed her that first day in Erica's.

Her gaze lifted from his hands to his face. Lips drawn together, eyes intent, he concentrated on his task.

Feeling her watching him, A.J. glanced up. "I'm sorry. I know this hurts."

"Not too bad," she breathed, her voice low, unsure. "But aren't you...?" Her words trailed off.

The gentle motion of the washcloth slowed, then stopped. He looked at her. Concern deepened his eyes to jade green. Or maybe it was a trick of the lamp and firelight.

A puzzled frown pleated his brows. "Aren't I what?"

Except for the crackling of the fire the room was completely silent. Outside the thick white fog crowded in around the windows like a dense curtain. They couldn't see out and no one could have seen in. They could have been alone in the world.

That thought sent an exhilarating thrill through Shelby, followed by a sickening lurch of nerves. She wished for an instant that she had a candy bar to nibble on, but it wasn't candy she craved. It was A. J. Court. She brought such dangerous thoughts to a screeching halt and fought to remember what he had just said. "Aren't you going to yell at me?"

He shrugged and nodded toward her arm. "I think you've been through enough, but I would like to know why you bolted out of here."

"I need to get back to my shop," she told him, then gasped in pain as he maneuvered her arm carefully to check for further injuries.

He winced and made soothing noises as he smoothed his hand over her shoulder.

"Lindy will have the shop closed up long before the time we got back to Santa Barbara."

"My parents will be worried about me."

"Lindy will tell them you're safe with me."

Her face was very solemn as she looked at him. Safe? He had to be kidding, she thought, but the word Lynn had used to describe him served to snap Shelby out of the dangerous lethargy that was invading her mind.

"Oh, of course. Lindy will let them know, but don't you think we should be going now?"

Without answering, A.J. finished cleaning her scrapes and wrapped her upper arm in bandages that he had found in the bathroom. He dropped the cloth he had been using back into the basin and went out onto the front porch. After a few moments he returned, carrying her suede jacket and purse. "I'm sorry, Shelby. The fog is so thick I can hardly see the car from the bottom of the steps. I almost had to crawl around on the ground to find these," he said, indicating her things. "We'll have to stay here all night." He laid the two articles on the table and gazed at her regretfully.

She would have been more upset if she thought he'd done this on purpose. But they were caught in circumstances they couldn't change. "I guess it can't be helped," she said, gaining a quick look of approval from him. "Do you suppose there's any food around here?"

He laughed. "That a girl, back to normal already."

She gave him a haughty look, made slightly ridiculous by her outsize shirt and bandaged arm. "I do not appreciate comments about my appetite."

"Then you shouldn't have such a big one," he retorted cheerfully, going to the pantry and pulling out several cans. "We've got a choice here. Chili, chili, and oh, yes, chili."

"Why don't we have chili?"

A.J. weighed a can in each hand. "Another piece in the puzzle of the secret life of Sanford and Sharon Altman."

Their gazes caught. Shelby had a mental picture of Mrs. Altman wearing the sexy gown and eating a huge bowl of chili. She giggled. When A.J. asked, "What do you suppose *he* wore?" she knew he was thinking the same thing. She collapsed into laughter while A.J. dug out a can opener, checked the fuel in the stove and lit the burner.

"You're very good at that," she complimented him, when he had carefully adjusted the flame.

"My mother cooked on one of these for years," he said in the offhand tone he always used when he mentioned his childhood.

Shelby thought about it for a few minutes and decided that he didn't resent his childhood or bemoan it. He accepted it as part of his past and used it to make himself a success. She felt a surge of admiration for him.

In a few minutes the chili was bubbling in the pan, and A.J. had dug out a box of crackers that were only slightly stale. He also found an unopened bottle of wine.

"Ah…" He smiled in satisfaction. "We'll dine well tonight."

"You really know how to show a girl a good time," Shelby said, batting her feathery lashes ingenuously. "First McDonald's, then homemade chili from a can. No man will be able to live up to the standards you've set." She struck a queenly pose against the sofa cushions. "You've spoiled me."

"That's not true." He ladled the chili into bowls. "Our first date—the day we met—I fed you some of the best food in Santa Barbara."

His face was so bland, as he took crackers from the box, that she thought she had imagined his slip of the tongue. "That was on the house. Besides, you would have kicked me out if you could have."

"True," he conceded with no apparent twinge of conscience. "Do you want to eat over there or can you come to the table?"

"I can come," she said, struggling up and favoring her sore knee. "Although, I could become accustomed to being waited on."

"You plan to fall downstairs pretty often?"

"Never again," she answered fervently.

The canned chili was good and filling, and the wine was delicious. They lingered over their meal and talked about whatever came to mind. Books, movies, sports…and they found their tastes were very similar.

A.J. pushed away his bowl. "What do you think about doing dishes?"

"I never think of it," she said airily. "That's why I never learned to cook. I was the one who always had to do the dishes. Plus, my arm is hurt."

He sent her a look that said "A likely story."

While she settled on the sofa before the fire, he cleared the table and piled the dishes in the sink, then brought the last of the wine and their glasses. "We might as well finish this off. It won't be any good the next time someone comes up here."

He sat beside her and lifted his wineglass to view the color. Backlighted by the fire, the wine looked like melted rubies. "Shelby, it's wonderful being with you tonight," he said quietly, taking her completely off guard. The glass began trembling in her hand.

He gazed at her. One side of his darkly handsome face was softly lit by the fire, the other was in deepest shadow. His angled cheekbones made interesting outlines in the half-light. She had the strange feeling, looking at only half his face, that she was seeing all of him for the first time.

He was strong but caring, wise but witty, harsh but gentle. It didn't seem to matter now that they had butted heads at every encounter, that he had tried to buy her off and make her quit.

Because she was in love with him.

The realization brought a surge of delighted awareness, followed by sickening dread. This wasn't right. She started to get up from the couch, not sure what she intended to do, but his hand shot out to stop her.

"Where are you going? It's too early for bed."

"I—I, uh, I don't know." Despair closed her throat on the words she should say. Words about needing sleep, going home tomorrow, finding Lynn, taking care of her business . . .

"Sit still." He pulled her down beside him. "Hey, are you thinking about the way I talked to you this afternoon? I admit I acted like a jerk."

He slipped his arm around her and gave her a friendly hug.

Shelby shivered, turning toward him. Her wide eyes and long lashes bespoke innocence, while the look she gave him was one of very feminine awareness.

His face was only inches away, his lips a mere whisper from hers. She thought of the time he had kissed her, and ached with longing. The invitation couldn't have been more obvious.

A.J.'s arm tightened and he lifted his other one to feather his fingers through her short curls. "I apologize." His voice was suddenly very husky, as if he was having trouble getting the words out or forgetting what he meant to say.

"Apologize? For what?"

"For...oh, never mind." He slid his hand around to clasp the back of her head and closed the gap between their lips. If she had thought their first kiss, weeks ago, had been overwhelming, this one was earth-shattering. His lips moved on hers with a thoroughness that left her gasping.

He kissed her again and again, murmuring low, unintelligible words to her. The sound of his voice was as exciting and hot as his lips on her mouth...her eyes, cheeks and ears.

"There's a word for a woman like you," he murmured against her throat.

"What is it?" she gasped, head thrown back, her face suffused with joy.

"Zaftig."

She turned her face to kiss him. Her husky laugh puffed against his cheek. "Doesn't that mean plump?"

"It means exciting, rich, fulfilling...ah, Shelby, why didn't I see you before?"

She wanted to clutch him to her and at the same time push him away. She felt the need to clasp her arms over her chest to stop the tingling that had started there. But she could do nothing about the heavy wanting that settled low in her body. There was only one satisfaction for that. A satisfaction she could never have.

Why hadn't he seen her before what? Before becoming engaged to Lynn?

Panicked sanity finally urged her to jerk away from him. She gasped in pain when she twisted her injured arm. "Don't, A.J. We mustn't do this. You're *engaged* to one of my oldest friends!"

She leaped to her feet but stumbled when her knee gave way. He was beside her in a flash, reaching to help, but she backed away. His face was as stricken as hers. He ran a shaking hand through her disarranged hair. "Shelby, let me explain. This has gone on long enough...."

"Never mind," she commanded, holding her hand out in front of her, her face confused and full of self-loathing. "Don't make it any worse than it already is!"

She turned and ran into the bedroom, threw herself across the bed and burst into tears.

CHAPTER NINE

PALE SUNLIGHT eased its way into the room as if apologetic for disturbing the woman who had spent such a tortured night. Shelby rolled onto her back and forced her gritty eyes open.

After crying for what seemed like hours she had fallen asleep in her clothes. Her elegant suede skirt would probably never be the same.

She would never be the same.

The problem with making a dramatic exit, she decided, was that one had to get up and face the same problem in the morning. And what a problem it was. She had fallen in love with another woman's fiancé. And the other woman happened to be one of her best friends.

Shelby threw her arm over her eyes and indulged in some well-deserved self-loathing. Her only consolation was that, for once, she hadn't plunged headlong into something. It had taken her weeks to make this particular dreadful mistake.

She heard A.J. stirring about in the other room, so she got up, carefully nursing her stiff, sore arm and knee and slipped into the bathroom where she used some makeup and a hairbrush to make what repairs she could to her ravaged face. Even the expensive cosmetics Lynn and Mrs. Altman had left behind couldn't disguise her puffy eyes and red nose, though. She smoothed as many wrinkles as she could from her skirt and tucked in the outsized T-shirt. She felt at least partially ready to face A.J.

He was in the kitchen area and when he heard her open the bedroom door, he spoke without turning around. "Coffee's ready. I'm not very hungry, but help yourself to what food there is. I think I'll take a shower before we start back."

His voice sounded perfectly normal but when he turned around, Shelby saw his face was as drawn and grim as her own. "Thank you, but I'm not hungry." At any other time he probably would have teased her, but now he just nodded, barely looking at her.

While he showered, Shelby took a cup of coffee and limped outside, where she anxiously scanned the sky. The fog had cleared somewhat so it was possible to see several yards in front of her. The visibility was good enough for them to be able to get out safely, she decided with relief.

She was intent on getting home but dreaded the thought of riding for four hours with A.J. She wished fervently that she could be like Dorothy in *The Wizard of Oz* and click her heels together three times in order to be instantly home. Unfortunately things like that didn't happen in the real world.

Back inside the cabin she saw that A.J. had washed their dishes from the night before. She cleaned up their coffee things and made sure the cabin was as neat as they had found it. A folded blanket on the end of the couch told her where A.J. had spent the night. Briskly, she picked up the blanket and headed for the cedar chest by the window.

Just before placing it inside she gave in to temptation and buried her nose in the scratchy wool. She imagined that it was still warm from his body, still filled with his indefinable masculine scent. Tortured thoughts and forbidden longings forced her to wrench the blanket away and stuff it into the chest. She slumped onto the chest and stared bleakly out the window. The angle of light reflected her face back at her. Her expression was every bit as anguished as she felt.

She smoothed her face into blankness and stood up quickly when A.J. emerged from the bedroom. His hair was damp and he was rolling the sleeves of his wrinkled shirt up to his elbows. He glanced around swiftly. "You shouldn't have cleaned up," he grumbled. "I would have done it. How is your arm? And knee?"

"Fine." She avoided his eyes, leaning over to pick up her jacket and the tattered blouse.

"Let me see," he said from right behind her. His fingers were gentle as he touched her puffy knee then grasped her elbow and checked her wounds. "The swelling should go down soon. It'll be all right. Looks like I got all the splinters, too."

His hand was warm on her arm, his thumb tender on the inside of her elbow, his scent was that of soap. Their eyes met. His were as anguished as her own but held a longing that shook her. Trembling, she pulled away and stepped back.

He didn't move. "Shelby." His voice was suddenly hoarse. "We've got to talk."

Horrified, she scurried toward the door. "No, there's nothing to talk about. We'd better go."

"Shelby!"

The look she gave him said the discussion was closed. His lips thinned for a moment in displeasure, but he followed her outside. After locking the door, he put the key back in its unsafe hiding place.

As they pulled away, Shelby gave one last glance at the cabin. Her feelings about it had undergone a radical change. Happy girlhood memories had been forever changed to ones of embarrassment and pain.

Once they got out of the lingering fog, A.J. drove fast, and Shelby was happy to have him do so. His face was set and tension was as thick between them as the fog had been around the cabin. If she had dared to, Shelby would have closed her eyes and pretended to sleep, but he was driving so fast she was afraid to take her eyes off the road.

He swung through town and pulled in at Spanish Court where Shelby had left her car. When A.J. stopped the Jaguar, she almost tumbled out onto the sidewalk in relief.

"Shelby, wait." A.J.'s voice was low and urgent.

She had stopped, halfway out of the car, with her back to him. Slowly, she turned her head to look back over her shoulder. "What is it?"

"About last night . . ."

Her thick lashes fluttered down over eyes dark with misery. "Don't talk about it."

"We've got to."

"It never happened."

"It did."

"It *shouldn't* have."

A.J. gripped the steering wheel and clenched his eyes shut. "Dear God, I don't know *what's* happened. Things have gotten so damned complicated. Listen, Shelby," he pleaded, opening his eyes. "I want to apologize. . . ."

"Don't." Her voice wavered and her blue eyes were huge and hurt as she backed out of the car. "Don't say anything more." Somehow having him apologize would make it even worse.

"Wait—" he called after her, but in an instant Shelby was out of the car, clutching her things to her, limping through the mall.

"SHELBY, I COULDN'T believe it when Alex told me the two of you had gone running off to the cabin looking for me." Lynn Altman swept into Featherstone Brides. Her print skirt swirled around her in a rainbow of colors as she pushed the door shut against a brisk fall breeze.

With a jerk Shelby turned toward her friend. She had been sunk in thought, her mind on an endless treadmill of guilt and embarrassment. The cold day hinted at the coming winter rains and the dreary sky reflected her own mood.

After returning home she had asked her mother and Lindy to take care of the shop for her that day. She had spent the remainder of Saturday and all day Sunday in her room, wallowing in guilt. She had mentally swung between plans to pretend that nothing had happened to ones that called for her to sell the business and leave town—maybe even join the Peace Corps. Her father would have told her the problem was within herself and that she couldn't escape herself.

So on Monday morning she had gotten up, dressed in her blue silk dress, a little loose now since she had barely eaten in three days, and had come to work.

Now, facing Lynn, she felt a fresh surge of guilt. Telling herself that nothing had happened didn't help. She had *wanted* something to happen.

"Good morning, Lynn. I guess it sounds pretty silly for us to have done that."

"Alex said it was his idea and that he dragged you along. How's your arm, by the way?"

Good grief, how much had A.J. told her? To her surprise, Lynn didn't seem jealous. Shelby wondered how much Lynn really loved A.J. if it didn't bother her for him to go off for the night with another woman. She squashed that last thought. There was enough on her conscience already.

"It's fine," she replied with a brittle smile. "Just a little sore."

Lynn tilted her head. "I thought it might be hurting. You look pale."

"It's the light in here." Shelby turned away to pick up the bookkeeping ledger she had been working on. "It makes me look ghastly. Anyway, *you* should talk. You don't look as if you spent a very restful weekend."

"I went up the coast to a hotel. To...think." Lynn's deep brown eyes were darker than ever as she gazed at Shelby then looked away.

Shelby took a deep breath. "Lynn, Carlo Rosetti was here Thursday."

Lynn didn't meet her eyes. "I know."

"So he *did* contact you?"

"Yes."

"He asked me about A.J. He was jealous and angry when he left here."

Lynn's soft mouth curved in a smile that Shelby had never seen there before. It could only be described as smug. "I know," she said again, then her smile faded. "He called me. We talked." She seemed to drift off into her own thoughts.

Appalled, Shelby gaped at her friend. "Then what happened?"

Lynn started out of her dreamy look. "Happened? Why, nothing. We still don't see eye to eye."

Why would she want to? Shelby wondered. She was going to marry someone else so why care about Carlo's opinion? "Lynnie, I don't know exactly what's going on—" boy, was that an understatement! "—but do you think you should be having anything to do with Carlo when you're going to marry A.J.? And what about your mother? Mrs. Moran thinks she's going to be really hurt if you don't involve her in the wedding plans."

Lynn's normally sweet and amiable face drew into a stubborn frown. "Is your mother here?" she asked, pointedly changing the subject.

Shelby sighed. "In other words, mind my own business." She wagged a finger at Lynn. "Just remember this wedding *is* my business. Mom and Lindy will be coming soon."

Lynn looked nonplussed and looked as if she was going to explain, but apparently changed her mind. "Good. I want to discuss our gowns. You look wonderful in that shade of blue," Lynn said, indicating Shelby's dress. "I think that's the color we should use for your bridesmaid gown. We'll have three in that shade and three in a lighter tone. Don't you think that sounds beautiful?"

A wave of sick dread began to churn in Shelby's stomach. She just couldn't be a bridesmaid for Lynn, but neither could she hurt her by refusing.

She was saved from replying by Mary and Lindy, who bustled into the shop carrying Karla Barnes's gown. "Shelby, I can't wait until we have the back room fixed up as a sewing area. I'm tired of sewing at home and dragging things in here." Mary panted out her familiar complaint while smiling a greeting at Lynn. "Is something wrong?" Her bright gaze darted from one girl to the other.

"No." They spoke in unison, then exchanged self-conscious glances. "We were just talking," Shelby went on. "Are you ready? Karla will be here soon."

While they waited for her to arrive, Mary sat down and began sketching a bridesmaid dress as Lynn talked about what she wanted. A gown with classic, flowing lines formed beneath Mary's flying pencil.

The bell toned quietly just as Mary was finishing one sketch. Distracted, Shelby looked up and froze when she saw that it was A.J. He came in quietly and shut the door, then turned to look at Shelby.

In the background, Lindy and Mary were discussing Lynn's dress, with a few quiet comments coming from Lynn herself. The classical music Shelby kept on the radio made a suitable background accompaniment. Outside, a raucous group of teenage girls skittered by, freed from school for the day, looking for boys, busy trying to impress each other.

Shelby heard none of it. She looked into A.J.'s face and saw exhaustion and pain to match her own. Her gaze was fixed on him, and she thought her heart had lurched into her throat and got stuck there, until she realized that she had merely forgotten to breathe. She gasped for air.

He walked toward her slowly. Panicked, Shelby backed away and he stopped, his face grim.

"Hello," he said quietly, as one would talk to a high-strung mare. "I came to pick up Lynn."

"Yes—" Shelby's voice broke and she cleared her throat. "She'll be ready in a minute. They've been discussing the gowns. Very... elaborate."

"How have you been?"

His low, sincere tone almost undid her. One part of her wanted to throw herself into his arms and cry out her troubles. Another more rational part was horrified that she could even think of such a thing. "I'm fine," she answered, her voice as empty as her heart.

She was lying, and they both knew it. A.J.'s black brows pulled into a frown. Before he could speak, Lynn emerged from the fitting room. "Why, Alex, I didn't know you were coming by."

He drew his eyes slowly from Shelby's pale face, leaving her to lean gratefully against the desk. She looked up to see her mother and sister following Lynn. The concern on their faces drew her up, and she fixed a smile on her lips.

A.J. walked over and kissed Lynn's cheek. She smiled briefly. "I thought we could have a drink if you're finished here," he said. "I got a phone call today that we've got to talk about." He shot a guarded glance at Shelby.

"All right. I just have to pay Shelby." Lynn drew out her checkbook and made her first payment to Featherstone Brides. A.J. watched with a frown.

Lynn said goodbye and allowed A.J. to take her arm as they moved toward the door, her eyes scanning the slip of paper in her hand. She turned back and held up the receipt, bewilderment and humor on her lovely face. "Is this a joke, Shel? A receipt signed by Shelby Court?"

"WAS THAT A FREUDIAN SLIP?" Lindy carefully folded Karla Barnes's gown back into its carrying bag and zipped it shut.

It was closing time. Mary had gone home casting worried glances at her youngest daughter.

"What do you mean, Lindy?" Shelby asked. She had her back to her sister, busily working on her system of keeping track of her clients' needs.

She had developed a flow chart to keep track of her clients and their arrangements. At any time she could look at the various colored lines of yarn on the board attached to the back room wall and know exactly what needed to be done. She had spent the last ten minutes standing and staring at the merging lines of the Altman-Court wedding.

"You know what I mean. That receipt you wrote for Lynn. The way you signed your name."

"Don't be silly," Shelby answered, busily moving a yellow section of yarn to a place where it had no business. "I simply miswrote my name."

"For the first time since you were four."

"I didn't mean to," she defended herself quickly, still avoiding Lindy's gaze. "We were talking, and I wasn't paying any attention to what I was doing...."

"When you were a little girl, you always talked very fast whenever you were lying. Nathan does the same thing. It's a dead giveaway."

Trembling, Shelby stopped shoving tacks onto the board and dropped her head forward, squeezing her eyes shut.

"You're in love with him, aren't you?"

"Yes...." Her voice was barely above a whisper.

"I saw it coming." Lindy took her sister into her arms. "From what Mom and Dad tell me the sparks flew between you from the very beginning."

Shelby drew Lindy's arms around and snuggled into the protection of her embrace. She began sobbing. "I feel like such a traitor! What kind of woman falls in love with her friend's fiancé?"

"A human one, darling." Lindy comforted her, patting Shelby's back. "A very human one, and if I know you, nothing further happened. You wouldn't have let it."

"But I wanted it to. Dad has always told us to follow our feelings. Our first reaction is usually our best one."

"That's right."

"Well, my first reaction was to..." Her voice trailed off. Even to a sister as understanding as hers, one didn't admit such a thing.

"Let him make love to you?"

Embarrassed, she nodded against Lindy's shoulder.

"No, honey. Your first reaction was to do the decent thing, which I'm sure you did."

"That's cold comfort," she sniffled.

Lindy rocked her gently back and forth. "I know, baby. I know."

"WHAT DO YOU THINK of this one?" Shelby asked.

With no thought to possible grass stains on her yellow skirt, she sank onto a small hillock overlooking a stream that meandered through the center of Sandrock Park. Sighing, she took off her three-inch-heeled pumps and rubbed her aching feet. She and Lynn had been searching out the perfect wedding site. Sandrock was the third park they had visited that day, along with two churches and a particularly beautiful section of beach.

Shelby had searched all the locations out months ago and had a list of several more. She was loathe to show the list to Lynn, though, for fear she would insist on seeing each one. If every detail of this wedding wasn't perfect, it wouldn't be because Lynn hadn't tried.

Lynn thought Shelby's slip of the pen the previous day was funny. She had arrived at the shop this morning full of plans to find the perfect spot for her wedding and when Lindy came in to watch the shop, she had swept Shelby out with her. Shelby enjoyed being with Lynn as much as ever, but she couldn't get thoughts of A.J. out of her mind.

Shelby struggled with jealousy. Lynn, who had always been quiet and amenable, had become animated and determined, even vivacious in the past few days, while Shelby had become withdrawn and pensive. Strange, Shelby thought with deep shame, being in love with the same man affected them in exactly opposite ways.

"This is perfect," Lynn finally decided, twirling around in an excited pirouette. "This is exactly what I want." She came back to Shelby and plopped down contentedly. "Now," she added under her breath. "If I can just get the groom to see it my way."

Shelby looked around at the towering candle-tip pines and huge oak trees spreading over the rolling hill of grass. The wind was sighing, making the trees sway and sing, rippling the grass as if a giant hand had passed over it. "A.J. will love it here, don't worry."

Lynn smiled, lowering her lashes slyly over sparkling brown eyes. "I'm sure he will. We're all going to look so lovely. Me in your mother's most beautiful creation, you in a gorgeous blue gown. Alex in a tuxedo and frilled shirt, walking down the aisle...."

An incredible pain knifed through Shelby and she sat up suddenly. "This place doesn't have an aisle," she snapped, unwillingly peeved at the image of A.J. and Lynn together. Ashamed, she reached for her shoes and slipped them on. Out of the corner of her eye she saw a movement and glanced to her left. She gasped and drew back as Carlo Rosetti rushed out from behind a wide-trunked oak.

"So—" he said, contemptuously. "This is where you are going to marry Alexander Court!"

Lynn, who had been half dozing on the grass, lost in her happy daydream, leaped up with a shriek. Shelby scrambled up beside her.

"Carlo! What are you doing here?" they gasped in unison.

Carlo stalked across the grass in short quick strides. His handsome face was twisted with anger and passion. "I have been following you as you have gone from place to place, finding the perfect spot for your marriage," he shouted, mimicking Lynn savagely.

"You've been listening to everything we said," Lynn accused, raising a shaky finger and pointing at him.

"Yes, and I'm tired of listening, tired of watching you make plans to marry this—Court." He practically spat out A.J.'s name as he reached out to grab Lynn's arm. Although he and Lynn were almost the same height, he seemed to loom over her. In contrast to Lynn's elegantly tailored pantsuit, he was dressed in old jeans and a T-shirt. His muscles flexed like steel cords as he drew the stunned blonde toward him.

Shelby leaped to Lynn's defense. "Let go of her, Carlo."

"Stay out of this, Miss Featherstone," he growled, without turning his head.

"I won't," she said, grabbing on to his arm. It felt like iron and would probably be as difficult to pry loose, she thought. Lynn wasn't helping at all but was staring at Carlo, wide-eyed. Shelby looked around frantically for help. The park was deserted. There were no early afternoon picnickers, no mothers strolling with small children, or soccer-playing schoolboys darting across the grass.

"You ran away from me last week," he said to Lynn, ignoring Shelby completely. "I wanted to talk to you."

Lynn opened her mouth but all that came out was, "I—Carlo..."

"Can you blame her?" Shelby sputtered. "You charged out of my shop like a bull and hunted her down. You probably scared her out of her wits."

Carlo shook Shelby off as casually as if she was a leaf clinging to his forearm. His dark eyes bore into Lynn's. "*Did* I frighten you?"

She shook her head, her face becoming pink. "Not—not really."

Carlo's voice was low and intense when he spoke again. "I came after you. I wanted to talk to you—I still want to—about Alex Court." His face grew anguished, his black eyes full of pain. "I know he is not good enough for you."

"Not good enough for her!" Shelby exclaimed, flabbergasted. "Why, I'll have you know he's a won-

derful man! He's good and thoughtful—but tough,"
she admitted for fairness' sake. "He came from pov-
erty and made himself a success." Shelby tossed her
short brown curls, her eyes blazing like star sapphires. "He has compassion and understanding
and—" Her tirade stumbled to a halt as she realized
that Lynn was staring at her, openmouthed.

"Why, Shelby," she gasped. Understanding seemed
to rush over her. "I had no idea."

Mortified, Shelby stared back at her friend. Now
her secret was out. She had betrayed their friendship
completely.

Shelby held out a shaky hand, hoping that Lynn
could forgive her. "Lynn, I'm . . . sorry. I never meant
to hurt you."

"Shel," Lynn gasped, "I never suspected. I've been
so blind."

Carlo's eyes darted from one girl to the other, and
he smiled with sudden determination.

He whirled Lynn around and forced her to look at
him. His dark eyes snapping, he said, "You're coming with me."

Chin up, Lynn faced him. "You know what I
want. . . ."

Carlo's face was suddenly so fierce, Shelby thought
he might strike out. She took a protective step toward
Lynn, who didn't flinch at the look on his face.

"You mean marriage."

"That's right."

Shelby gasped, but the two combatants ignored her.

They stared at each other, eyes battling. Finally, he
nodded. "If that's what it takes."

He grabbed Lynn's left hand and snatched off her
engagement ring. She squealed in surprise and jerked

her hand back as Carlo shoved the solitaire at Shelby. "Here, give this back to Court. Lynn won't be needing it."

Still holding on to Lynn, Carlo began running. Lynn took leaping strides to keep up.

"Hey, wait a minute!" Shelby, who had been frozen into immobility, snatched up her purse and started after them. The combination of high heels and a sore knee slowed her too much, though. Carlo, dragging Lynn with him, soon disappeared over the next hill in the direction of the parking lot.

By the time Shelby reached the bottom of the next hill, they were roaring away in Lynn's white Triumph, with Carlo driving. "Call Alex!" Lynn yelled out as they sped away.

Shelby stared, astounded that Lynn was eloping with Carlo and telling *her* to break the news to A.J. She turned in a helpless circle, grasping Lynn's ring in her hand. Lynn had driven them to the park, and now she was stuck with no car. A black Corvette was still in the parking lot, and Shelby decided it must belong to Carlo. Why hadn't he taken his own car and left her the keys to Lynn's? Shelby fumed. Because he wanted to strand her, of course, she concluded.

With an angry snort, she headed down the road to the nearest phone, which was at least a mile away.

SHELBY CLUTCHED her purse, with Lynn's ring inside, and reached up to knock on A.J.'s front door. She had intended to call him as Lynn had said, but somehow she didn't feel right about it. It seemed tacky to call a man on the phone to tell him his fiancée had just eloped willingly with another man! Some things had to be said in person.

She had called Sienna who had hurried over to pick her up and take her to the shop. When she'd phoned A.J.'s office, Miss Simmons had said he'd left for the day. With her sister's puzzled and insistent questions following her, Shelby had rushed out to her car.

How was she going to break the news to him? Possible explanations and apologies had formed in her mind as she drove but when A.J. swung the door open and stood staring down at her, her mind went blank.

He had removed his suit jacket and loosened his tie. Obviously, he had just run distracted fingers through his hair because the black tendrils were mussed, standing on end.

"Shelby." His lips formed her name, as his green eyes took a quick, thorough, catalog of her features. "What's wrong?"

She didn't know what she was going to say. He looked awful, his face drawn into lines that added years. Surprise crossed his face, and then he began to smile. Sick dread churned in her stomach because she knew that momentarily she would be responsible for taking that smile off his face. "May... may I talk to you?"

He stepped back, swinging the carved door wide. "Of course. Come in."

She stepped into a greenhouselike entryway. It was lit by a skylight and full of lush plants. He led her through it into a living room furnished with an over-stuffed contemporary sofa and chairs in rich earth tones.

He indicated the sofa. "Sit down. Would you like something to drink?"

Miserably, she shook her head. "A.J., this isn't a social call. I have something for you...."

The eager delight on his face faded to a wary regard. "What is it?"

With shaking hands she reached into her purse and pulled out the ring. Her words tumbling over each other, she plunged into a recounting of the afternoon's events.

Robotlike, A.J. extended his hand as he listened. She dropped the ring into his palm and watched his fingers curl over it.

His stunned look brought tears spurting to Shelby's eyes. Oh—she could just kick Lynn and Carlo for hurting him like this!

"...and they took off in Lynn's car. I don't know where they've gone. A.J., I'm so sorry." Her hands fluttered to her face. Through her muffling fingers, she sobbed, "Lynn wasn't fighting him at all. She *wanted* to go—insisted that he marry her."

A.J. pulled Shelby into his arms and comforted her. She sobbed on his crisp white cotton shirt for long minutes. Eventually she began to realize that his chest was heaving up and down beneath her cheek.

Pity and love overwhelmed her and she wrapped her arms around his waist, offering what comfort she could. "A.J., I'm so sorry. I can't believe Lynn and Carlo did such a thing!"

He didn't answer, and it was several more seconds before Shelby realized that he wasn't crying at all—but laughing!

Shocked, she jerked her tear-streaked face back and stared up at him.

"Thank God they did," he gasped, his eyes bright with tears of laughter. "I didn't know how much longer I could go on with this!"

CHAPTER TEN

FOR A MOMENT, Shelby thought he might be hysterical, but to her profound amazement, she realized that he was truly happy and relieved.

She tried to bring her scattered thoughts into line. Finally she managed to say, "I'm—glad you're taking it so well."

She drew away, rummaging in her purse for a tissue to wipe her eyes while A.J. struggled to get control of himself. Her surprise and shock at his reaction were giving way to embarrassment at her own.

When his laughter had finally wheezed to a stop and he stood, hands on hips, grinning down at her, she said, "Let me get this straight. You're not upset that your fiancée eloped with another man?"

He drew a deep breath and expelled it in a long sound of relief, looking happier than she had ever seen him.

"I would be," he said, "if she had really been my fiancée."

Shelby gaped at him. She was silent for a full minute before gasping, "What do you mean?"

A.J.'s amusement faded when he saw how pale her face had become. He took her arm, led her toward the sofa and forced her to be seated. "Sit down. I'd better explain."

She flounced onto the couch. "Yes. You'd darn well better!"

He filled his lungs with a deep breath and flexed his shoulders as if somehow he felt suddenly lighter. "It's a long story."

"And getting longer by the minute...."

Shelby's irate expression and pinched mouth told him she was in no mood for delays. "You already know how I fooled Erica," he began. "You were in on it—"

Shelby frowned. "What's this got to do with Mrs. Martinez?"

He held up his hand. "I'm getting to that. Lynn and I had an agreement. She was supposed to help me trick Erica. That's why the ring was in the napkin." He pulled the ring out of the pocket he had dropped it into and turned it around in his fingers. "The plan was for her to slip it on as soon as she got there, to make it look as if we were already engaged, had been planning marriage for a while."

Involuntarily, Shelby's right hand covered her left, as she remembered the brief time she had worn the ring.

"The ring belonged to my mother," he said and added wistfully, "It was the first thing of value my dad ever bought after the farm started making a profit. I kept it for my wife to wear." He watched her rubbing the third finger on her left hand.

Shelby saw his eyes on her and laced her fingers together.

"Anyway," A.J. went on, "Lynn was going to help me and I would pose as her fiancé to get Carlo's attention."

Shelby started to speak, but he held up his hand. "Let me finish—" his dimple quirked up "—and then you can yell at me." He paused and began pacing across the room. "My idea was that if Lynn and I just leaked word of our engagement, if Lynn even suggested she was considering marrying someone else, Carlo would come around. Oh, I know, her parents, especially her mother, didn't like him. And Carlo thought she deserved to marry a rich, successful man. But Lynn was determined to have *him*."

Shelby jumped up, clamped her hands onto her hips and stalked up to him. "Then why that big announcement at Lynn's welcome-home party? *That* was certainly more than a 'suggestion' that you two were going to marry."

A.J. spread his hands wide. "Because Anderson was there. Lynn couldn't locate Carlo, so . . ."

"She was trying to flush him out," Shelby concluded, pursing her lips.

"Yes, I had no idea you and Lynn were close friends until later. I thought you had ingratiated yourself with her to get me to change my mind about Spanish Court." A.J.'s hand sliced the air. "Hell, I tried to get you to leave the party. Do you know what I was thinking while we were dancing?"

Shelby shook her head briefly, her expression distrusting.

"Right woman . . . wrong moment. I wanted to get to know you, but the timing stank. You are the most exciting—troublesome—thing to ever come into my life. I wanted to get the business with Lynn over with fast so I could concentrate on you."

Seeing the wistfulness on his face, hearing words she had never expected to hear, Shelby almost softened toward him, but she stiffened her resolve. She had suffered guilt and remorse—for nothing!

"You could have told me the truth later," she pointed out angrily. "Lynn was acting so strange I didn't know what to think. You were trying to buy me off—make me quit. Why?"

"Because I thought exactly this kind of thing would happen. Carlo isn't the type of man to get dressed up in a monkey suit and get married in front of five hundred of Lynn's nearest and dearest friends. I told her that, but she was looking at the whole thing through rose-colored glasses. She wasn't supposed to plan a real wedding at all."

"But you and Carlo had never met. How do you know he wouldn't want a big wedding? You don't know his personality...." Shelby closed her eyes briefly and sighed. "You had him investigated, didn't you?"

"Hell, yes," A.J. growled without revealing a shred of conscience. "She was my best friend's daughter. I couldn't let her marry some jerk. Carlo turned out to be a good man, if somewhat hardheaded."

Shelby took a turn around the room, her steps short and angry. "But why didn't you tell *me* what was going on? It wasn't fair to keep me in the dark like that. All kinds of plans were in motion...."

"I know." His gaze slanted down guiltily. "But I had promised Lynn I wouldn't tell *anyone* the truth until Carlo saw reason. Then, after the night in the cabin, I almost told you, but you wouldn't listen."

She barely heard him, caught up in her own anger. "Lynn manipulated him—and you manipulated me!" She jabbed a thumb at her own chest.

"Try to understand—I was caught in the middle!" A.J. insisted. "Lynn didn't want her mother to know she had gone behind her back."

Shelby flung her hands wide. "The fake engagement was announced in every newspaper in two counties. How did you two think Mrs. Altman wouldn't see it? Surely friends contacted her?"

A.J. shook his head. "Her sister is living with her. All her calls are screened. Sharon hasn't been the same since Sanford's death. It hits some people that hard." He paused and ran his hand over his jaw. "Sanford's death is what convinced Lynn to go all out for Carlo."

Shelby spun to face him. *"What?"*

"She decided life was too short to spend it away from the man she loved."

Shelby shook her head as if she had received a severe blow. "She's changed so much. I don't know what to think. All these big plans—and today...running off like that..." Her words trailed off as her eyes accused him. "Last weekend when we went to their cabin—she was probably with Carlo, wasn't she?"

His hands flew up and out. "Yes, but I swear I didn't know about that until later. She didn't contact me at all. As far as I knew, she was still 'engaged' to me. I really was worried. Rosetti is pretty hotheaded." He paused when her distrustful expression didn't change. "All right—I admit I probably could have driven out of that fog, but I wanted to be alone with you. But it seemed like things went from bad to worse." His voice grew husky. "But lord, how I wanted you."

Shelby shook her head. "But you knew it was all a farce—and my business, my reputation was at stake. It wasn't fair to keep this from me!"

He took a step toward her. "I know, but by yesterday I began to see that things were going to work out. Carlo called and threatened me."

Shelby gasped, "What?"

A.J. shrugged. "Jealous threats not serious ones. I had a feeling he would do something soon." He seemed to dismiss the other man. "Then, at your shop, when you signed that receipt Shelby Court, I knew there was hope for us."

So many conflicting thoughts were buzzing around in her head that she couldn't think. She flinched at the memory of what she had written on Lynn's receipt, then lifted her hand and rubbed the back of it against her forehead. "Do you have any idea what guilt I went through?" she burst out. "I agonized—hated myself—because I had fallen in love with my friend's fiancé!"

When she realized what she had just admitted, her hands flew to her mouth as if she could call the words back. Her eyes were huge, peeking over the tips of her fingers. Turning, she fled the room, heading toward the front door, appalled at what she had just blurted.

A.J. was after her in a flash. "Don't run away from me, Shelby!" He caught her at the door and spun her into his arms. "Hell, what a way to tell a man that you love him," he muttered, his green eyes dark and fervid, his voice intense. "But I should have expected it from you."

His mouth came down on hers and Shelby forgot that she was supposed to be angry with him. Passion flared between them, and she wound her arms around his neck, remembering only that she loved him.

He broke away, breathing hard, and placed his forehead against hers. "Whatever happened to your family philosophy of 'Go with your feelings'? I thought if you loved me, you would have said so days ago."

"I couldn't. There was Lynn."

"I love you, Shelby," he said. "I thought this mess would never be straightened out so I could tell you that."

She snuggled into his arms, savoring his words, relieved and delighted that the barriers between them were finally down. "I was sure I would never hear *you* say *that*." Her hand stole up to pinch him hard on his ear.

"Ouch!" he yelped. "What was that for?"

"For deceiving me and making me agonize and hate myself for loving you."

His expression grew suspiciously innocent. "I never actually lied to you. There were just certain things I couldn't tell you."

She gave him a haughty look. "Don't let it happen again."

"I promise." He paused, his eyes solemnly searching her face. "Now I want a promise from you."

"What?"

He lifted the solitaire. "Marry me."

Shelby's eyes filled with tears as she stared at the diamond and then at him. "Marry you?"

"You've got most of the plans made, don't you?"

"Plans?" Shelby couldn't seem to stop parroting his words.

"For the Altman-Court wedding—now the Featherstone-Court wedding." When she didn't speak, he rushed on. "Hey, is it the ring? I can get another one. I can understand why you wouldn't want to wear one that someone else had worn, and—"

She stilled his quick words by standing on tiptoe to kiss him. "This ring will do fine." Her face was very grave as she said, "It was always mine, A.J."

He grinned suddenly and lifted her hand, slipping the ring on easily and kissing the place where it rested. "Yes, it was, wasn't it? And now it even fits."

CHAPTER ELEVEN

"I'VE BEEN WAITING for this for years," Erica Martinez said. After the toasts were made and the cake was cut she approached the bride and groom slowly, leaning on her cane. Now she stood holding Shelby's hand lightly.

A.J., looking unbelievably handsome in a black tuxedo, his arm around Shelby's waist, grinned at the older woman. "We've each kept our part of the bargain, Erica. You look wonderful, better than you have in years."

It was true, Shelby saw. Erica's eyes were bright and clear. Her face had lost its slight puffiness and her breathing sounded clearer.

Erica flushed with pleasure then lifted her eyebrows curiously. "And you're now a safely married man. I began to wonder, though, Alexander...."

"Wonder?" He and Shelby exchanged quick glances. "About what?"

"Those strange notices in the newspaper."

Shelby bit her lip. "The newspaper?"

Erica's glance darted from one to the other of the newly married couple. "I had the Santa Barbara paper sent to me while I was at Lake Tahoe."

"Oh?" A.J. asked, his face wary. "You did, huh?"

"Yes. And I saw something about your engagement to a Lynn Altman. Sanford and Sharon's daughter. But I knew that couldn't be true. You've always treated her like a little girl. And besides, you were already engaged to Shelby...right?''

A.J. looked distinctly uncomfortable and Shelby couldn't hide her grin. She looked down, arranging the folds of the simple, elegant white satin gown her mother had created for her.

"Um, right.''

"I just knew it wasn't true,'' Erica said, her eyes shrewd. "There I was, no cigarettes, no salt on my food for weeks, eight glasses of water *a day*. I was sure you wouldn't have tricked me into such misery. Especially after Carmen said you called up and spent an hour raving about Shelby. How exciting, how full of life she was.''

Shelby threw her husband of one hour a startled look.

A.J. shook his head. His face was as sober as a supreme court justice, but his green eyes were twinkling devilishly. "Me trick you, Erica? We had a bargain and we both kept our parts, didn't we?''

Releasing Shelby's hand, Erica reached up to hug A.J. who returned the gesture. "Yes. I'm so proud. I wish your parents could have seen this day.'' She turned back to Shelby. "They would have liked you.''

Shelby smiled tremulously. "I'm glad.''

Erica moved away, and Shelby said out of the side of her mouth, "Do you think she knows the truth?''

A.J. slid her a downward glance. "She sure does.''

"Do you think she minds?''

"Nah, she got what she wanted.''

"What was that?''

"Me married off.''

'Do *you* mind?''

Ignoring the three hundred people crowded into the reception hall A.J. turned and slid his arms around Shelby's waist. Tilting her head back he kissed her long and hard. Cameras flashed and the guests whistled their approval.

"What do you think?'' he asked when he let her up for air.

She gasped, grabbing for the circlet of gardenia buds nestled in her short curls. "I think you love me.''

He kissed her again. "You think right. And I'm damned grateful you didn't make me wait too long to get married.''

The day of his proposal—and Lynn's elopement—had been less than a month ago. Their wedding plans had been hurried, but thorough. Shelby's family had all pitched in, showing the teamwork that was the foundation of Featherstone Brides.

She sighed blissfully. "I'm sorry Lynn and Carlo couldn't be here, but I guess Rome isn't exactly across the street. She sounded so surprised when she called to say she received the wedding invitation.''

"I don't know why,'' A.J. said dryly, "considering the way I was panting after you. But, then, she was so involved in trapping Carlo, she couldn't see anything else that was going on.''

"From what I hear he doesn't seem to mind being trapped.'' Shelby leaned back and looked up at him with a teasing smile, sure of his love. "Panting, hmm?''

"Like a marathon runner.'' A.J. swept her into his arms for the dance that was just starting. "But I'd better get used to it. I have the feeling you're going to lead me a merry chase for the rest of my life."

She fluttered her lashes down over innocent blue eyes. "I'll do my best, darling."

Harlequin American Romance

**Romances that go one step farther . . .
American Romance**

Realistic stories involving people you can relate to and care about.

Compelling relationships between the mature men and women of today's world.

Romances that capture the core of genuine emotions between a man and a woman.

Join us each month for four new titles wherever paperback books are sold.
Enter the world of American Romance.

Amro-1

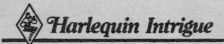

Harlequin Intrigue

Two exciting new stories each month.

Each title mixes a contemporary, sophisticated romance with the surprising twists and turns of a puzzler... romance with "something more."

Because romance can be quite an adventure.

Romance, Suspense and Adventure

Harlequin Superromance

**Here are the longer, more involving stories you
have been waiting for...Superromance.**

Modern, believable novels of love, full of the complex
joys and heartaches of real people.

Intriguing conflicts based on today's constantly
changing life-styles.

Four new titles every month.
Available wherever paperbacks are sold.

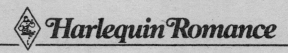

Harlequin Romance

Coming Next Month

#2965   NO GREATER JOY   Rosemary Carter
Alison fights hard against her attraction to Clint, driven by
bitter memories of a past betrayal. However, handsome,
confident, wealthy Clint Demaine isn't a man to take no for
an answer.

#2966   A BUSINESS ARRANGEMENT   Kate Denton
When Lauren advertises for a husband interested in a businesslike approach to marriage, she doesn't expect a proposal from a
handsome Dallas attorney. If only love were part of the
bargain....

#2967   THE LATIMORE BRIDE   Emma Goldrick
Mattie Latimore expects problems—supervising a lengthy
engineering project in the Sudan is going to be a daunting
experience. Yet heat, desert and hostile African tribes are
nothing compared to the challenge of Ryan Quinn. (More about
the Latimore family introduced in THE ROAD and TEMPERED
BY FIRE.)

#2968   MODEL FOR LOVE   Rosemary Hammond
Felicia doesn't want to get involved with handsome financial
wizard Adam St. John—he reminds her of the man who once
broke her heart. So she's leery of asking him to let her sculpt
him—it might just be playing with fire!

#2969   CENTREFOLD   Valerie Parv
Helping her twin sister out of a tight spot seems no big deal to
Danni—until she learns she's supposed to deceive
Rowan Traynor, her sister's boyfriend. When he discovers the
switch his reaction is a complete surprise to Danni....

#2970   THAT DEAR PERFECTION   Alison York
A half share in a Welsh perfume factory is a far cry from Sophie's
usual job as a model, but she looks on it as an exciting
challenge. It is unfortunate that Ben Ross, her new partner,
looks on Sophie as a gold digger.

Available in March wherever paperback books are sold, or
through Harlequin Reader Service:

In the U.S.
901 Fuhrmann Blvd.
P.O. Box 1397
Buffalo, N.Y. 14240-1397

In Canada
P.O. Box 603
Fort Erie, Ontario
L2A 5X3

Keepsake

Harlequin Books

You're never too young to enjoy romance. Harlequin for you . . . and Keepsake, young-adult romances destined to win hearts, for your daughter.

Pick one up today and start your daughter on her journey into the wonderful world of romance.

Two new titles to choose from each month.